OXFORD WORLD'S CLASSICS

THE LIFTED VEIL • BROTHER JACOB

GEORGE ELIOT was born Mary Ann Evans on 22 November 1819 near Nuneaton, Warwickshire, on the Arbury estate of the Newdigate family, for which her father was agent. At the age of 9 she was imbued with an intense Evangelicalism that dominated her life until she was 22. Removing to Coventry with her father in 1841, she became acquainted with the family of Charles Bray, a free-thinker, and in 1844 was persuaded to translate Strauss's *Life of Jesus* (3 vols., 1846). After her father's death in 1849 she spent six months in Geneva, reading widely. On her return she lived in London in the house of the publisher John Chapman, editing the *Westminster Review*. Around 1852 she met George Henry Lewes, a versatile journalist, whose marriage was irretrievably ruined but divorce impossible. In 1854 she went to Germany with him for nine months, and for the next twenty-four years lived openly as his wife. Through his encouragement at the age of 37 she began to write fiction. Four stories, serialized in *Blackwood's Magazine*, and reprinted as *Scenes of Clerical Life* (1858) under the *nom de plume* George Eliot, were an instant success. *Adam Bede* (1859) became a best seller; *The Times* declared that 'its author takes rank at once among the masters of the art'. In *The Mill on the Floss* (1860) and the five novels that followed, George Eliot, with increasing skill, continued the subtle probing of human motive that leads many modern critics to regard her as the greatest novelist of the nineteenth century. Lewes's death in 1878 was a devastating blow that ended her career as a novelist. On 6 May 1880 she married John Walter Cross, a banker twenty years her junior, and on 22 December died at 4 Cheyne Walk, London.

HELEN SMALL is Fellow and CUF Lecturer in English Literature at Pembroke College, Oxford. She is the author of *Love's Madness: Medicine, the Novel, and Female Insanity, 1800–1865* (1996) and *The Long Life* (2007), and co-editor of, and a contributor to, *The Practice and Representation of Reading in England* (1996). She has edited several nineteenth-century novels, including Walter Besant's *All Sorts and Conditions of Men* and (with Stephen Wall) Charles Dickens's *Little Dorrit*.

OXFORD WORLD'S CLASSICS

GEORGE ELIOT

The Lifted Veil
Brother Jacob

Edited with an Introduction and Notes by
HELEN SMALL

OXFORD
UNIVERSITY PRESS

OXFORD
UNIVERSITY PRESS

Great Clarendon Street, Oxford OX2 6DP

Oxford University Press is a department of the University of Oxford.
It furthers the University's objective of excellence in research, scholarship,
and education by publishing worldwide in

Oxford New York

Athens Auckland Bangkok Bogotá Buenos Aires Calcutta
Cape Town Chennai Dar es Salaam Delhi Florence Hong Kong Istanbul
Karachi Kuala Lumpur Madrid Melbourne Mexico City Mumbai
Nairobi Paris São Paulo Singapore Taipei Tokyo Toronto Warsaw

and associated companies in Berlin Ibadan

Oxford is a registered trade mark of Oxford University Press
in the UK and in certain other countries

Published in the United States
by Oxford University Press Inc., New York

Editorial material © Helen Small 1999

Database right Oxford University Press (maker)

First published as an Oxford World's Classics paperback 1999

British Library Cataloguing in Publication Data

Data available

Library of Congress Cataloging in Publication Data

Data available

ISBN-13: 978-0-19-283295-5

7

Typeset by RefineCatch Limited, Bungay, Suffolk
Printed in Great Britain by
Clays Ltd, St Ives plc

CONTENTS

Introduction   ix

Note on the Text   xxxix

Select Bibliography   xl

A Chronology of George Eliot   xliii

THE LIFTED VEIL   I

BROTHER JACOB   45

Explanatory Notes   88

H. É. Blanchon, *La Transfusion du sang* (1879). By kind permission of the Bibliotèque Nationale

INTRODUCTION

Much of the impact of 'The Lifted Veil' derives from a powerful final scene which is discussed in this Introduction. Readers who do not wish to have the shock of the ending spoiled should treat the Introduction as an Afterword.

IN H. É. Blanchon's painting *La Transfusion du sang*, exhibited at the Paris Salon in May 1879, the dramatic climax of 'The Lifted Veil' was startlingly depicted for the French public.[1] The Salon catalogue, necessarily, provided an explanatory key:

A young and celebrated doctor, friend of M. ***, attempts a transfusion, with his own blood. The operation succeeds and the dead woman is revived. In this brief flash of life, she recognizes Mme *** who has just entered the room, and 'unveils' her guilt: 'You plan to poison your husband' she cries.

George Eliot, *The Lifted Veil*[2]

Blanchon's interpretation of the scene is superbly histrionic. In the centre of the canvas the maid (Mrs Archer) rears up in bed. Head craned forward, nightgown slipping from her shoulders, she thrusts an accusing finger at Bertha, who shrinks away to the front left of the canvas. To the right of the reanimated corpse a bewhiskered Charles Meunier in a long white surgical apron is arrested in dismay, pressing his finger to his forearm to staunch the bleeding from the opened vein. Assisting him, but almost lost in the shadows, is the inscrutable figure of Bertha's husband, Latimer.

---

[1] I am grateful to Professor John House of the Courtauld Institute for showing me a slide of the painting from his personal collection. I am also indebted to Tim Farrant, Kate Flint, John Lyon, Sheila Stern, Paul Taylor, Alison Winter, and my editor, Judith Luna, for their assistance in the preparation of this edition.

[2] A fairly free translation. The full French text read as follows: 'Blanchon (Henri-Émile), né à Paris, élève de M. Cabanel.—Rue Jadin, 5. 306—*La transfusion du sang*. Un jeune et célèbre docteur, ami de M. ***, fit, avec son propre sang, un essai de la transfusion. L'opération réussit et la morte se ranima. Dans cet éclair passager de la vie, elle reconnut Mme *** qui entrait dans la chambre, et dévoila sa culpabilité: < Tu veux empoisonner ton mari! > lui cria-t-elle. . . . George Eliot, *The Lifted Veil*.' *Explication des Ouvrages de Peinture . . . des Artistes Vivants, Exposés au Palais des Champs-Elysées Le 12 Mai 1879* (Paris: Imprimerie Nationale, 1879), 26.

The painting is now sadly lost, though a black and white photograph of it—reproduced on p. vii—survives in the Bibliothèque Nationale, Paris. George Eliot knew of the work's existence (a friend sent her the catalogue entry for the exhibition[3]), but never saw it, so one can only speculate about how she would have responded. In principle she seems to have found the idea comically un-English: 'I call this amusing—I ought rather to have said typical of the relation my books have with the French mind'; and (to another friend), 'Perhaps [the transfusion scene] hits the dominant French taste more than anything else of mine.'[4]

For all Eliot's comparative stylistic restraint her subject-matter was undeniably lurid and it is not surprising that she worried about how 'The Lifted Veil' would be received. At the end of March 1859 she wrote to her publisher, John Blackwood, alerting him to the story's existence and offering it for publication in *Blackwood's Magazine* (generally known as *Maga*): 'I have a slight story of an outré kind—not a *jeu d'esprit*,' she noted, 'but a *jeu de melancolie*, which I could send you in a few days for your acceptance or rejection as a brief magazine story.'[5] The tentativeness of the offer must have been surprising. *Adam Bede*, Eliot's first novel, published in February of that year, had been a huge critical success. Speculation was rife about the identity of its author and, as Blackwood himself was fully aware, most magazines in the current climate 'would give any money for a scrap with George Eliot's name attached'.[6] Even so, her hesitancy was unmistakable. Drawing on the support of the man she lived with and called her husband, G. H. Lewes, she added: 'I think nothing of it, but my private critic says it is very striking and original, and on the strength of that opinion, I mention it.'[7] Blackwood was encouraging, and 'The Lifted Veil' was duly posted to him on 29 April—accompanied by a cover note, 'Herewith the dismal story'.

Blackwood took over a fortnight to reply, and even then had to be prompted to do so by Lewes. When he did at last respond on 18 May

[3] *The George Eliot Letters*, ed. Gordon S. Haight, 9 vols. (New Haven: Yale University Press, 1954–78) (hereafter cited as *L*), vii. 163.
[4] *L* vii. 163, 165.
[5] *L* iii. 41.
[6] *L* iii. 112 n. 6.
[7] *L* iii. 41.

it was clear that he was in something of a quandary. 'It is a very striking story,' he wrote, 'full of thought and most beautifully written. [But] I wish the theme had been a happier one, and I think you must have been worrying and disturbing yourself about something when you wrote.' He found the transfusion business in poor taste and, though the quality of the writing (and, no doubt, the desire to keep Eliot on board) persuaded him to publish, 'strongly advise[d]' her to delete the scene.[8] Eliot held her ground nevertheless (as she usually did when presented with editorial criticism) and the story appeared uncut in the July 1859 issue of *Maga*. John Blackwood had his way on the question of a signature, however, rejecting Lewes's suggestion that the name 'George Eliot' appear at the end. It was not *Maga* policy to print the author's name, and this was not a case for which Blackwood would be keen to make an exception. He informed Major William Blackwood, his brother and partner in the business, that he had told Lewes and Eliot it would be 'better not to fritter away the prestige which should be kept fresh for the new novel. . . . I daresay I am the only editor who would have objected to the name in the present furor.'[9]

When the first responses from readers came in they were, predictably, mixed. 'Lovers of the painful are thrilled and delighted', Blackwood reported; 'others like me are thrilled but wish the author in a happier frame of mind.'[10] Many years later, Eliot's friend and acolyte Edith Simcox replied less tactfully when Lewes quizzed her about the story in Eliot's presence: 'I was put out by things that I didn't quite know what to do with—it was a shame to give such things a moral, but—'.[11] Until the early 1980s, when Beryl Gray published first a ground-breaking essay on 'The Lifted Veil' and Victorian 'pseudo-science', followed by a Virago edition of the story, Simcox's view seems to have been shared by the great majority of critics. The story was in the main neglected, on occasion frankly disparaged. In the past decade, however, it has come to be one of Eliot's most widely read and discussed works. Not least, it is now celebrated as the nearest Victorian successor to that more famous horror-story about scientific experimentation with death and life, Mary Shelley's *Frankenstein*

---

[8] *L* iii. 67.
[9] *L* iii. 112 n. 6.
[10] *L* iii. 112.
[11] *L* ix. 220.

(1818). The young Latimer, like Frankenstein, travels to Geneva—
once the home of Rousseauean Romanticism and in the 1850s still
one of Europe's great centres for physiological research. Like
Shelley, Eliot portrays philosophical conflicts but also, more deeply,
an alliance between art and science. 'The Lifted Veil' is also the
nearest nineteenth-century English parallel to Edgar Allan Poe's
macabre tale of mesmeric revivification, 'M. Valdemar' (1839). Yet
another possible influence can be found in James Hogg's uncanny
novel about psychological splitting and doubling, *The Confessions of
a Justified Sinner* (1824). But however much Eliot's story shares
with these and other Gothic fantasies, it remains, centrally, a work
of mid-Victorian realism, its power stemming largely from Eliot's
recognition that scientific inquiry was making available in the
1850s a radical extension of what 'the real' might be seen to
include.

In 'The Lifted Veil' Eliot takes more risks with narrative voice,
with narrative structure, and with the taste of her readership, than
she ever would again. The story deserves admiration for the scope
and power of its writing. It also, however, demands to be read as a
fiction firmly rooted in its historical moment. Like Gray, many
readers and critics have been struck by the dark fantasy Eliot weaves
around some of the more contentious branches of physiological and
psychological research in the period—mesmerism, phrenology,
experiments in revivification, research into the 'double brain'. Her
personal encounters with phrenological and mesmeric practice and
her extensive reading in physiological theory inform Latimer's
relentlessly medicalizing narrative of his life, and 'The Lifted Veil'
cannot be properly understood without examining those sources in
some detail. Yet this story is also, and relatedly, Eliot's anatomy of
her own moral philosophy. Latimer is the only artist protagonist in
her fiction but he fails to produce a single work of art, becoming
instead the vehicle for an extraordinary pathologization of the ideals
one finds elsewhere in Eliot's work. Keen and sympathetic insight
into others provides, in the absence of a conventional Christian faith,
the moral foundation for all her great novels. Each of them promotes
that insight by means of an omniscient, though often ironizing, narrative voice. In 'The Lifted Veil', however, authorial omniscience is
recast as a first-person narrator's diseased and reluctant knowledge
of the workings of other minds. Through Latimer's thwarted and

increasingly misanthropic sensibility, Eliot pursues the answer to questions she would never again allow herself to confront so unprotectedly: Would sympathy necessarily accompany keenness of insight? More fundamentally—and the question addresses both literature and science—what are the proper limits of our desire to see into our own condition?

While still a student in Geneva Latimer is taken seriously ill and, as he gradually begins to convalesce, discovers that his sickness has wrought a change in his mental state. He becomes prey to two forms of clairvoyance. One compels him to see into the future, including the manner of his own death. Hence one of the most arresting opening paragraphs in Victorian fiction: '. . . I foresee when I shall die, and everything that will happen in my last moments.' Beginning his autobiography, as he will end it, bitterly awaiting his impending heart attack, Latimer makes an immediate challenge to the conventions of realist narrative. Though the narrative frame encloses a cogent, linear plot, it forecloses narrative progression, depriving the reader, as Latimer himself has been deprived, of the freedom not to know what will happen.

Latimer's second mode of clairvoyance forces him to endure a painful insight into the minds of the people around him.

I began to be aware of a phase in my abnormal sensibility, to which, from the languid and slight nature of my intercourse with others since my illness, I had not been alive before. This was the obtrusion on my mind of the mental process going forward in first one person, and then another, with whom I happened to be in contact: the vagrant, frivolous ideas and emotions of some uninteresting acquaintance—Mrs Filmore, for example—would force themselves on my consciousness like an importunate, ill-played musical instrument, or the loud activity of an imprisoned insect. (13)

The voice is unlike any other in Eliot's work, and in using it she was making considerable demands on a *Blackwood's* readership not, in recent years, used to being so challenged. The style acts as a mirror for Latimer's 'double consciousness'. It is oddly neutral, scrutinizing itself from a distance ('I began to be aware of a phase in my abnormal sensibility') yet warped by emotion.

But this superadded consciousness, wearying and annoying enough when it urged on me the trivial experience of indifferent people, became an intense pain and grief when it seemed to be opening to me the souls of those who were in a close relation to me—when the rational talk, the graceful attentions, the wittily-turned phrases, and the kindly deeds, which used to make the web of their characters, were seen as if thrust asunder by a microscopic vision, that showed all the intermediate frivolities, all the suppressed egoism, all the struggling chaos of puerilities, meanness, vague capricious memories, and indolent make-shift thoughts, from which human words and deeds emerge like leaflets covering a fermenting heap. (13–14)

Latimer's loss of his poetic idealist's faith in the potential nobility of the human mind strips 'The Lifted Veil' of almost any imaginative sympathy with the experiences of others. Most of the other characters—his brother Alfred, Bertha (Alfred's fiancée and, after Alfred dies in a hunting accident, Latimer's wife), their neighbours and friends—are in consequence thinned out. His father escapes only because Latimer deliberately shuns him, their 'radical antipathy' making insight into his mind, until he is broken by Alfred's death, a peculiarly intolerable 'affliction'. Charles Meunier retains a rather bland integrity because he re-enters the story when Latimer's insight is in abeyance—and because it is necessary to Eliot's plot that Meunier as scientist should repeat Latimer the artist's loss of innocence. Watching the ghastly results of his transfusion experiment, Meunier is 'paralysed; life for that moment ceased to be a scientific problem to him' (42).

Latimer's vision into the workings of the mind invalidates his own understanding of character. The social behaviour from which, for him, a concept of the whole person emerges is stripped away to reveal a seething confusion of pettinesses and complications. It would be easy for modern critics to misread this as a Victorian anticipation of post-structuralism: an 'emptying out' of the convenient fiction promoted by most nineteenth-century novels, that character is a coherent composition of thoughts, words, and actions. That claim would do an injustice both to the Victorian novel and to Eliot's idea here. This is, in principle, not an emptying but a filling out of the mental and moral life. Where it goes wrong is that Latimer believes he sees everything, when in fact his knowledge is partial—forensic, without the saving presence of sympathy. Moreover, for all his self-absorption, he never really turns the insight back on himself. His narrative strips others of their rationality, grace, and wit, but he retains the necessary coherence of a savage indignation.

'So absolute is our soul's need of something hidden and uncertain', he tells us in one of the few passages in which Eliot allows him to speak with lyrical poignancy (or, more accurately, allows herself to take over his voice),

that if the whole future were laid bare to us beyond to-day, the interest of all mankind would be bent on the hours that lie between; we should pant after the uncertainties of our one morning and our one afternoon; we should rush fiercely to the Exchange for our last possibility of specula- tion, of success, of disappointment; we should have a glut of political prophets foretelling a crisis or a no-crisis within the only twenty-four hours left open to prophecy. Conceive the condition of the human mind if all propositions whatsoever were self-evident except one, which was to become self-evident at the close of a summer's day, but in the mean- time might be the subject of question, of hypothesis, of debate. Art and philosophy, literature and science, would fasten like bees on that one proposition which had the honey of probability in it, and be the more eager because their enjoyment would end with sunset. Our impulses, our spiritual activities, no more adjust themselves to the idea of their future nullity, than the beating of our heart, or the irritability of our muscles. (29)

This is the necessitarians' nightmare proposition that, if we could know everything there is to know about our present moment, we would, like Laplace's God, know everything that will happen here- after. In the 1850s the necessitarian doctrine, or 'determinism' as it was beginning to be called, was attracting new interest among philo- sophers and experimental scientists, particularly on the Continent, where questions about the extent to which our actions are pre- determined by our motives, desires, and beliefs, or indeed by our physiological make-up, were closely debated.[12]

For everyone but Latimer in 'The Lifted Veil' free will remains a basic assumption, and speculation a constant attraction. Latimer's

[12] See Ian Hacking, *The Taming of Chance* (Cambridge: Cambridge University Press, 1990), 150–9, on the emergence of determinism's modern meaning of 'the doctrine of necessity' in the 1850s.

father is a successful banker whose choice of education for his difficult younger son is explicitly a gamble, the result of a 'recent
interest'—presumably financial as well as intellectual—in 'mining
speculations' (Eliot's oblique reference to the new scientific education being promoted by Huxley and others at the Government
School of Mines in Jermyn Street, London). Alfred too is a betting
man. In Vienna, Latimer is left to stroll alone in the gardens of
the Lichtenstein Palace,[13] while the rest of the party goes to the
Belvedere gallery 'to settle a bet which had arisen between my
brother and Mr Filmore about a portrait' (19). But for Latimer, once
cursed with clairvoyance, a single mystery remains: the opaline
mind of Arthur's fiancée, pale blonde, 'fatal eyed' Bertha. She is
his embodiment of what Nietzsche called 'the enchantment of
woman'.[14] She is not, however, allowed to enchant the reader, who is
from the first made aware of the coolly sarcastic streak in her nature,
the 'cruel eyes'. If she doesn't fully function for us as a character, it
is not only because Latimer's portrait of her as a girl is tainted by his
knowledge of what she will become but because his investment in
her seems an intolerable burden of responsibility to be borne by an
18-year-old girl.

Latimer's account of the slow stripping away of hope and the
uncertainty he connects with Bertha is compelling enough as a story
of desire, but with some knowledge of 'The Lifted Veil's' extensive
debt to Victorian science it becomes immensely richer. From his
early account of an attack of blindness in childhood onwards,
Latimer is presented both as a man of sensibility for our (increasingly alienated) sympathy and as a clinical case-study for our more
objective contemplation. Mr Letherall, the phrenologist, is the first
to lend medical authority to Latimer's father's sense that he has 'an
odd child', tracing the shape of the boy's skull with his thumbs to
determine his intellectual, emotional, and moral faculties. He diag-
noses a 'deficiency' in those parts of the brain which determine the
capacity for orderliness, calculation, and punctuality, and an over-
development of the faculty of 'ideality' (according to the leading
nineteenth-century British promoter of phrenology, George Combe,

---

[13] Eliot mistakenly refers to it as the Lichtenberg, a suburb of Berlin.
[14] *Beyond Good and Evil*, trans. R. J. Hollingdale, with a new introd. by Michael
Tanner (Harmondsworth: Penguin, 1990), 169.

'a manner of feeling and of thinking, befitting the regions of fancy more than the abodes of men', essential to the make-up of poets and artists).[15]

As Beryl Gray has pointed out,[16] George Eliot had a long-standing interest in phrenology. She read Combe's *Elements of Phrenology* (1824), and in July 1844 had a cast made of her head by James Deville of the Strand for her friend, and in some degree mentor, Charles Bray, a passionate believer in the new science. After mis-identifying the cast as that of a man, Combe analysed Eliot's head in person in August 1851, declaring her 'the ablest woman whom I have seen', with 'a very large brain', 'great analytic power and an instinct-ive soundness of judgment'. Soon after this, however, she made the acquaintance of G. H. Lewes, whose undisguised scepticism about the scientific claims of the British phrenologists and their European precursors Gall and Spurzheim seems to have given something of a jolt to her ideas. By 1855 Bray was accusing her of having lost faith in the 'physiological basis' of phrenology.[17] Lewes published an extended critique of the subject in the revised edition of his *Biographical Dictionary of Philosophy* (1857), and Bray promptly gave Eliot notice that he would be retaliating in print, which he did in the revised edition of his *Philosophy of Necessity* (1863).[18]

This fracas between two men so close to her must have caused her embarrassment if not distress, but she put the disputed 'scientificity' of phrenology to work in 'The Lifted Veil', using it to underwrite, but at the same time leave a vital question mark over, Latimer's 'morbidity' of mind. Does the evidence of his skull reveal an inher-ent and ineradicable predisposition to mental disorder? Or does phrenology rather impress upon us the plasticity of his mental life, its potential redirection through education? Combe repeatedly stressed the power of schooling to stimulate and direct the adaptive powers of the mind; Mr Letherall's prescription of a strict diet of science is, on the other hand, signally unsuccessful.

[15] G. Combe, *Elements of Phrenology* (Edinburgh: John Anderson, 1824), 69.
[16] B. M. Gray, 'Pseudoscience and George Eliot's "The Lifted Veil"', *Nineteenth-Century Fiction*, 36/4 (1982), 407–23. See also Rosemary Ashton, *George Eliot: A Life* (London: Hamish Hamilton, 1996), 3, 89, 54.
[17] *L* ii. 210.
[18] *L* ii. 402–3; and Ashton, *George Eliot*, 191. For further details see the Explanatory Notes, p. 90.

'The Lifted Veil' appears, in its discussion of Latimer's education, to be setting up an antagonism between the artist and the man of science. Such a conflict would have had strong reverberations for an audience alert to the rapid cultural and political advancement of the sciences in the mid-1850s.[19] As the story proceeds, however, Latimer becomes surprisingly willing to appraise himself in scientific or (though the word should be treated with caution) 'pseudo-scientific' terms.[20] His language repeatedly strikes the register, and often the precise terminology, of mid-Victorian physiology and pathology of mind: 'my diseased consciousness', 'in my face the stamp of a morbid organisation', 'my superadded consciousness'. Crucial metaphors are drawn from the field of scientific experimentation and vivisection:[21] he sees others' thoughts 'as if thrust asunder by a microscopic vision', observes weaknesses of character 'laid bare in all their naked skinless complication' (15). The range of scientific models, many of them running counter to each other (the 'stamp' on the physiognomy versus the revelation of what lies beneath the skin), is striking, and an important reminder that, for all its growing cultural and social power, 'science' was not a monolithic and clearly defined category, nor did it yet possess a sufficiently specialized vocabulary to ensure a straightforward reception by its audiences.

One phrase which illustrates this difficulty peculiarly well, and whose original connotations are likely to be lost on twentieth-century readers, is 'double' or 'divided' consciousness. For many Victorian readers versed in contemporary scientific debates, the term would have brought to mind mesmerism, or animal magnetism. Once again, Eliot had a close knowledge of the issues involved. In the summer of 1844 she had submitted to being partially mesmerized by W. B. Hodgson, Principal of the Liverpool Mechanics'

---

[19] See David Layton, *Science for the People: The Origins of the School Science Curriculum in England* (London: Allen & Unwin, 1973); and Alison Winter, *Mesmerized: Powers of Mind in Victorian Britain* (Chicago: Chicago University Press, 1998), ch. 11.

[20] The definition of science in this period was much less clearly fixed than it has become in the 20th cent. 'Pseudo-science' implies a view of phrenology and mesmerism as little more than quackery. In practice, though they were contentious, both enjoyed wide acceptance, and, at certain stages, strong institutional backing. Though the term science is not entirely satisfactory, tending to erase the constantly shifting boundaries of the category, it is generally preferable to the pejorativeness of 'pseudo-science'.

[21] See Richard Menke, 'Fiction as Vivisection: G. H. Lewes and George Eliot', forthcoming in *ELH*.

Institute—a liberal educationalist and friend of Bray. According to
Cara Bray he succeeded 'to the degree that she could not open her
eyes, and begged him most piteously to do it for her'.[22] She would also
have known of Wilkie Collins's series of articles in the *Leader*,
between 17 January and 3 April 1852. 'Magnetic Evenings at Home'
took the form of public letters to G. H. Lewes, describing a number
of soirées held at a Somerset house the previous Christmas, where
Collins had watched his host, a count, mesmerizing 'Mlle V', companion to the countess. Mlle was made to demonstrate clairvoyant
powers and, on one occasion, to respond to the suggestion that she
had eaten poison. Another time she 'cross-mesmerized' Collins, touching him and causing a tingling sensation in his hands. Lewes was
unconvinced of the validity of the observations, rebutting Collins's
claims with a robust letter to the *Leader* on 27 March entitled 'The
Fallacy of Clairvoyance'.[23]

'The Lifted Veil' was also clearly influenced by the work of one
mesmerist, the well-known William Gregory, Professor of Chemistry
at Edinburgh University and author of *Letters to a Candid Inquirer,
on Animal Magnetism* (1851).[24] Eliot first came into contact with
Gregory's experiments in the field when she corresponded with
Combe in early 1852. He told her of Gregory's claims concerning
the clairvoyant powers of mesmeric subjects. A particularly close
parallel to Latimer's experience is to be found in Gregory's reports
of a male patient who, when in a deep mesmeric sleep, saw
Cologne—a city he had never visited—'in a bird's-eye view, or as
from a balloon' and was able to give 'a most perfect description' of it,
as on other occasions he could of Bonn, various far-flung Eastern
cities, and ancient Greece.[25] Once again, Eliot does more than simply
replicate what she had read or heard report of. As Gray notes,
Latimer's vision of Prague (his first clairvoyant experience) distorts
the reality: his Prague is not the 'grand old city' Eliot described so

[22] See Gordon Haight, *George Eliot: A Biography* (Oxford: Clarendon Press, 1968),
54–5; Ashton, *George Eliot*, 54.
[23] G. H. Lewes, 'The Fallacy of Clairvoyance', *The Leader*, 27 March 1852, 305.
For discussion, see Winter, *Mesmerized*, 326–7.
[24] See Gray, 'Pseudoscience', 413–18; and Malcolm Bull, 'Mastery and Slavery in
The Lifted Veil', *Essays in Criticism*, 48 (1998), 244–61.
[25] William Gregory, *Letters to a Candid Inquirer, on Animal Magnetism* (1851),
147–8. Quoted in Gray, 'Pseudoscience', 417.

warmly in her journal account of her visit there in 1858,[26] but a 'thirsty' city with a river like a 'sheet of metal', the broad sunshine seeming to scorch the 'dusty, weary, time-eaten grandeur of a people doomed to live on in the stale repetition of memories, like deposed and superannuated kings' (9). His clairvoyance also distorts the mesmeric capabilites of another, much more famous individual cited by Gregory (but not noted by Gray). Alexis Didier, a clerk in a Paris haulage firm, was by far the greatest mesmeric celebrity of his day. He toured England twice with his mesmerist (the haulage firm's manager), J. B. Marcille—first in 1844–5, and again in 1849–50— and gave remarkable displays both of clairvoyant travel and of clairvoyant mind-reading.[27]

Malcolm Bull has argued that Latimer's 'sympathetic clairvoyance' (or mind-reading), as opposed to his 'direct clairvoyance' or 'clairvoyant prevision' (the terms are Gregory's), is the consequence of his having been magnetized by Bertha at their first meeting, when she fixes her eyes on him and he feels in response 'a painful sensation as if a sharp wind were cutting me'. 'Such instant rapport', Gregory noted, was often the product of a particularly marked difference in temperament, the stronger magnetizing and assuming power over the weaker. Latimer loses consciousness at precisely the point when (Gregory again) 'there is in many cases a veil, as it were, drawn before the eyes'. (That a man should be mesmerized by a woman was an inversion of the expected gender relation, though by no means an unprecedented one: Percy Bysshe Shelley and Wilkie Collins were among the more famous names to have found themselves in such a situation.) Thereafter Bertha's 'self-centred negative nature' exercises a 'tyranny' over his 'morbidly sensitive nature perpetually craving sympathy and support'. She alone resists his clairvoyance and only when he accepts his submission does he begin to gain insight into her and feel a corresponding weakening of her hold on him. Bull claims a parallel between Gregory's account of the disposition of power between mesmerist and mesmeric subject and Hegel's description of the master–slave dialectic (which chimes closely with Hegel's writing elsewhere about magnetism, known to Lewes). Initially overwhelmed by the superior will of the mesmeric

---

[26] *J* 324. See Explanatory Notes, p. 91.
[27] See Winter, *Mesmerized*, 143–6.

operator, the mesmeree—by his or her very subjection—begins to have insight into the mesmerist's mind and thus to redress the imbalance of power, just as Hegel's slave begins to emancipate himself only once he accepts his slavery.

Oddly, despite growing interest in Eliot's reworking of Gregory's findings, one of the closest mesmeric models for Latimer's experience has not yet been noted. Among Gregory's most frequently cited precursors in magnetic experimentation was the German natural philosopher Karl von Reichenbach, whose work in the mid-1840s on the similarities between mesmeric phenomena and the behaviour of crystals and magnets was later perceived by many to have anticipated Faraday's discovery of the polarization of light. In 1845 von Reichenbach described for the first time a category of subjects whom he called 'sick sensitives', whose bodies were highly responsive to the presence of magnetic or crystalline substances. Gregory published a short but much talked about English abstract of Reichenbach's claims in 1846, and in 1851 a full translation of the work.[28] Though Gregory's own researches would lead him to examine these phenomena in detail in relation to mesmerism, Reichenbach's 'sensitives' had not been mesmerized. They were, as the name suggested, individuals who, in a normal waking state, were highly responsive—indeed, pathologically responsive—to their environment, and they provide an alternative, more ambiguously 'mesmeric' model for understanding Latimer's condition.

Mesmeric ideas are evidently at work in Latimer's narrative, but it is, finally, less than clear how far they are being endorsed by Eliot and just where they begin and end. Part of the difficulty of assessing the impact of Victorian science on 'The Lifted Veil' stems from the fact that competing, and even incompatible, theories of the mind regularly shared the same language in this period. So, when Latimer tells us that he suffered from a form of 'double consciousness' he is using a semi-clinical term whose mesmeric application Bull, understandably, seizes upon. William Gregory used it to describe a state in which the mesmeric subject remained in possession of his or her normal waking consciousness while also experiencing the altered

---

[28] Karl von Reichenbach, *Researches on Magnetism, Electricity, Heat, Light, Crystallisation and Chemical Attraction: In Their Relations to the Vital Force*, trans. and ed. William Gregory (London: Taylor, Walton, & Maberly, 1850). For discussion see Winter, *Mesmerized*, 277–81.

consciousness produced by the magnetic sleep. The words had a different meaning for researchers into the organic structure of the brain. Sir Henry Holland, later Eliot and Lewes's friend and occasional consultant physician, was among those hypothesizing during the 1850s that the hemispheric structure of the brain (the 'double brain') could lead, in cases of injury or disease, to 'a sort of double-dealing' of the mind with itself as if there were 'two minds', one of which attempted 'to correct by more just perceptions, feelings, and volitions, the aberrations of the other'.[29] If one adopts Gregory's position, the phrase 'double consciousness' indicates powers or capacities of the mind, albeit unwanted. Holland offers a more pathological view of the case: Latimer as neurotic or hysteric.

To complicate matters further, Eliot's journals offer a case of her using the term 'double consciousness' in a way which should make us wary of treating either mesmerism or physiology of the brain as the exclusive key to Latimer's story. In her account of her visit to Italy in 1860, she uses the term more loosely, although she was certainly aware of its technical applications and perhaps intended to hint at them: 'One great deduction to me from the delight of seeing world-famous objects is the frequent double consciousness which tells me that I am not enjoying the actual vision enough, and that when higher enjoyment comes with the reproduction of the scene in my imagination I shall have lost some of the details, which impress me too feebly in the present because the faculties are not wrought up into energetic action.'[30] Similarly, Herbert Spencer noted in his *Autobiography* that she once told him she was 'troubled by double-consciousness—a current of self-criticism being an habitual accompaniment of anything she was saying or doing; and this naturally tended towards self-depreciation and self-distrust'.[31] 'Double consciousness' is, in short, a sufficiently transparent and malleable term to be able to slip between scientific and non-scientific meanings: it is both Latimer's self-diagnosis and his metaphorical

[29] Henry Holland, *Chapters on Mental Physiology* (London: Longmans, Brown, Green & Longmans, 1852), 185, 187. For discussion see Jane Wood, 'Scientific Rationality and Fanciful Fiction: Gendered Discourse in *The Lifted Veil*', *Women's Writing*, 3/2 (1996), 161–76.

[30] *J* 336.

[31] Herbert Spencer, *An Autobiography*, 2 vols. (London: Williams & Norgate, 1904), i. 396, quoted in Ashton, *George Eliot*, 220.

approximation to what his mental state felt like. To address the issue from a slightly different angle, Eliot has selected a range of mental phenomena, descriptive terms, and fields of knowledge which are sufficiently unstable in themselves and in their relations with each other to prohibit her readers from perceiving them as rigid old truths or as mere scientific gimmicks.

Criticism which seeks to weigh the relative importance to 'The Lifted Veil' of various strands in the ongoing debate that was Victorian science risks turning into a twentieth-century revival of their struggle for influence—the mesmerists and phrenologists v. the anatomists and pathologists of the brain. The important question is not their ranking in relation to one another, but what they hold in common. 'Science' means 'knowledge' (it is a direct derivation from the Latin *scientia*). However disputed their authority, however much they overlap or are in contention, all these fields of inquiry are seeking to lift the veil of ignorance from the inmost operations of our minds, hearts, and (it is Latimer's word) souls. Until the end of 'The Lifted Veil' those claims are in the main theoretical, but with the blood-transfusion operation Eliot makes a startling shift into a more invasive medical practice, and provides the novel with something like a summary statement of its dealings with science hitherto. It is less a 'totalizing metaphor'[32] than an organizing dramatic expression for the story's profound fear that the pursuit of knowledge may end by violating 'that doubt and hope and effort which are the breath of [the soul's] life'.

Before looking at the symbolic implications of the scene, it is important to note that it too has strong roots in contemporary experimental physiology. As Kate Flint has shown,[33] Eliot draws upon and imaginatively transforms Lewes's research into transfusion for his two-volume study of *The Physiology of Common Life* (1859–60) which was in mid-serialization in *Blackwood's Magazine* and about to appear as a book when Eliot began writing 'The Lifted Veil'. In his chapter on 'The Structure and Uses of Our Blood' Lewes gives a detailed account of the history of transfusion attempts,

---

[32] J. Hillis Miller, 'Optic and Semiotic in *Middlemarch*', in Jerome H. Buckley (ed.), *The Worlds of Victorian Fiction* (Cambridge, Mass.: Harvard University Press, 1979), 125–45 (p. 129).

[33] Kate Flint, 'Blood, Bodies, and *The Lifted Veil*', *Nineteenth-Century Literature*, 51/4 (1997), 455–73.

acknowledging the remarkable recent successes of James Blundell and Charles-Édouard Brown-Séquard in vindicating the procedure's viability (a series of disastrous transfusion operations had led to it being discredited and, in Paris at least, criminalized at the end of the seventeenth century, despite some early successes). Eliot evidently had a more detailed acquaintance with Brown-Séquard's transfusion experiments than Lewes's book alone would have provided, specifically a 'successful' operation to restore a heart-beat in a dog suffering from peritonitis. (The 'confounded animalicule', to quote John Blackwood's unfeeling phrase,[34] lived another five to six hours.)

   Blackwood was not the only one to find the influence of 'our excellent scientific friend'[35] (Lewes) undesirable for once. Even to more discerning readers, like Henry James, the transfusion drama has often seemed insufficiently worked into the rest of the tale.[36] George Eliot could undoubtedly have arranged the disclosure of Bertha's murderous designs with less strain on her plot, and without having to resort to Mrs Archer as an instrument with which to prise open the other woman's soul (the maid is only too clearly a stand-in for Bertha, the taste of the day tolerating a fictional account of surgery on a servant much more readily than on her mistress[37]). In fact, as Flint demonstrates, the transfusion scene is closely responsive to the rest of 'The Lifted Veil'. Knowledge of the workings of the human body and mind, of the nature of woman, of the nature, too, of authorship (Flint suggests that Eliot is in part expressing a perception that Victorian women had to draw on male authority in order to speak freely, as she herself did in adopting a pseudonym[38])—all these are brought together in the image of the male scientific hero infusing his life-restoring blood into a dead woman. The result violates

---

[34] *L* iii. 67.

[35] Ibid.

[36] Henry James, ' "The Lifted Veil" and "Brother Jacob" ', *Nation*, 26 (25 April 1878), 277, rpt. in Gordon S. Haight (ed.), *A Century of George Eliot Criticism* (Boston: Houghton Mifflin, 1965), 130–1 (131); and Ashton, *George Eliot*, 220.

[37] One might, of course, argue that she is also Latimer's stand-in, accusing Bertha (a woman they both come to loathe) in his stead.

[38] I extrapolate slightly from Flint's statement that 'this text functions as an experiment, among other things, in George Eliot's awareness of the complications involved in a woman author writing with masculine authority—whether one takes "masculine" in the sense of personal identity or dominant discourse' ('Blood, Bodies, and *The Lifted Veil*', 470).

the sanctity of death, the mystique of femininity, and many polite Victorians' sense of the limits of artistic taste.

There is a further, more fundamental engagement to be made here, not strictly with Lewes's science, so much as with his writing about the principles of scientific inquiry. The last chapter of *The Physiology of Common Life* was entitled 'Life and Death'. It opened with a discussion of vitalism—that is, the belief that there is a life-force independent of the organism. Lewes dismissed the doctrine with the (highly contentious) claim that it had, by 1859, been scientifically discredited but was still observably at work in the language and the 'metaphysical attitude of mind' of many physicians.[39] He urged on his readers a more philosophical acceptance that Life is unknowable, 'one of the great mysteries surrounding us'.

Having made up our minds on this point, having resigned ourselves to the complete relinquishment of all hypotheses, of all endeavours to penetrate into the inscrutable, we cease vexing ourselves with the arcana of Nature, and try to ascertain the *order* of Nature.

'There are minds', he conceded, 'which feel distrust at such resignation' and which fear the scientists' reduction of Life to a phenomenon of equivalent interest and accessibility to inorganic structures:

They seem to dread lest Life should be robbed of its solemn significance, in the attempt to associate it, even remotely, with inorganic phenomena. But this fear arises from narrow views of Nature. It is because reverence for Nature has not been duly cultivated; because familiarity with inorganic phenomena has blunted our sense of their unspeakable mystery.[40]

For Lewes the pursuit of scientific knowledge was sustained by reverence for the inherent mystery of all matter—organic and inorganic. In terms strikingly prohibitive of Latimer's experiences he insisted that 'The mystery which underlies all Existence cannot

---

[39] William Benjamin Carpenter, the leading physiologist of his generation, was the most prominent defender of the notion that there is a vital character to life which cannot be reduced to mere mechanism. Michael Faraday was another defender of the vital principle.

[40] George Henry Lewes, *The Physiology of Common Life*, 2 vols. (London, 1859–60), ii. 422–3.

be unveiled by us . . . All we are entitled to say is this—there is a *speciality* about vital phenomena; and this speciality must warn us against reasoning about them as if they were *not* special.'[41]

For Latimer, science eradicates mystery. The blood transfusion's results confirm the truth he has feared: there is nothing in death to redeem our miserable existence on this side of the veil. As he cries in horror after Mrs Archer expires a second time with her hatred and vengeance still unsatisfied, 'Great God! Is this what it is to live again . . . to wake up with our unstilled thirst upon us, with our unuttered curses rising to our lips, with our muscles ready to act out their half-committed sins?' (42). His entire narrative is, of course, silently predicated on the disappearance of God. Latimer's cry is not a prayer but a protest (interestingly, the original *Blackwood's* text had read 'Good God! This is . . .', with more the tenor of a prayer, but not the minimal openness of the rhetorical question). That spiritual despair is one more context for Eliot's revulsion against the ideal of complete knowing. Her break with organized Christianity notwithstanding, she would have agreed that if there is no mystery there is no God.

One mystery remains about the scene, for the reader at least. There is a puzzling excessiveness about Mrs Archer's condemnation of Bertha. To what is she referring when, having exposed the murder plot, she makes the further and more personal accusation against her that 'you laughed at me, and told lies about me behind my back, to make me disgusting . . . because you were jealous' (42)? Most readers will suspect a sexual drama, perhaps a shared attraction to an un-named man, but we have no further evidence for this. Its significance is precisely its unexplainedness. This is the one opacity allowed to remain in a narrative obsessed with the destruction of mysteries. For all its likely tawdriness it allows something to escape Latimer's sense that everything is known to him. It is, perhaps, a sign of how far he has lost his commitment to life that he does not even seem to notice it. The fundamental opposition in this story is not between art and science, or even between the ideal and the real, but between the fearful prospect of absolute knowing and the saving possibility of doubt and speculation. Hence, finally, the importance of Eliot's employment of science in ways which repeatedly provoke our

[41] Ibid. 424.

readerly speculation into Latimer's condition, but never offer us certain knowledge of it.

Not surprisingly, Eliot's biographers have been quick to find in Latimer's story evidence of her own anxieties about death. The composition of 'The Lifted Veil' was interrupted by the death of her older sister Chrissey in March 1859, by problems with her own (always erratic) health, and, more particularly, by Lewes's chronic illness. She had watched, panic-stricken, when he fainted in April 1855, believing him for some minutes to be dead.[42] (He fainted again three days after she submitted the manuscript of 'The Lifted Veil'.) It seems likely she had his physical frailty in view when describing Latimer's infirmity, though her protagonist's philosophy and temperament were the very obverse of Lewes's. Latimer's affliction with disease of the heart perhaps owes more to the recent medical history of her friend Herbert Spencer, another chronic sufferer in mind and body.[43]

More potent than the fear of death in 'The Lifted Veil', however, is the expression it gives to Eliot's familiarity with depression. From her teenage years she had suffered recurrent and debilitating periods of despondency in which she felt herself to be without sympathizers, and in which she became (as several of her correspondents found to their cost) intolerant of friends or suspicious of their loyalty. Praise, however warm, she often suspected of being insincere, whereas a hint of criticism would be taken to heart and brooded upon for days (hence Lewes's care to keep any adverse reviews from her).[44] 'I can't help losing belief that people love me', she wrote to Cara Bray in 1857, '—the unbelief is in my nature and no sort of fork will drive it finally out.'[45] Strikingly, she seems to have been particularly beset by fears around the time of writing 'The Lifted Veil' that she would be

[42] *L* ii. 199.
[43] Shortly after Spencer rejected Eliot's romantic interest in him in 1853, he resigned his post as sub-editor of the *Economist* and went travelling on the Continent for the good of his health. He was diagnosed as suffering from a cardiac disturbance, though he would in fact live another half-century. A few months later, while writing the section on 'Reason' for *Principles of Psychology*, he suffered a nervous breakdown not unlike that described in his Mill's *Autobiography* and not unlike some aspects of Latimer's illness. See Haight, *George Eliot*, 118–19.
[44] See Ashton, *George Eliot*, 164–5.
[45] *L* ii. 397.

unable to repeat the success of *Adam Bede*, reporting to William Blackwood in May 1859 that 'I *am* assured now that "Adam Bede" was worth writing—worth living through long years to write. But now it seems impossible to me that I shall ever write anything so good and true again. I have arrived at faith in the past, but not at faith in the future.'[46] All this makes Latimer's alienation from those around him, and his loss of a viable future, read like a nightmare extension of her own 'morbid' tendencies—as Rosemary Ashton puts it, 'a negative version of herself'.[47]

'Art must be either real and concrete, or ideal and eclectic', Eliot wrote to John Blackwood in July 1857.

> Both are good and true in their way, but my stories are of the former kind. I undertake to exhibit nothing as it should be; I only try to exhibit some things as they have been or are seen through such a medium as my own nature gives me. The moral effect of the stories of course depends on my power of seeing truly and feeling justly.[48]

That observation is at the heart of her expectations of herself as artist—and of her readers—and numerous similar statements could be winnowed from her letters, journals, and essays. But in 'The Lifted Veil', for the first and last time, she puts that artistic and ethical ideal fully to the test, asking what it would be like in practice to have so acute an understanding. How should we respond if compelled to see into every man or woman's 'equivalent centre of self'? Will art which offers a keen insight into the mental life of others necessarily deepen our humanity? Latimer is granted such insight and recoils from it, even as he taunts us, his readers, with our powerlessness to gauge *his* experience: 'Are you unable to give me your sympathy—you who read this? Are you unable to imagine this double consciousness within me . . . ? (21).'

There are moments of recognition in Eliot's novels that sympathy may, after all, be an inadequate basis for a moral code. Many of them are remarkable for their compensatory beauty of expression. So, in a famous passage of her most famous work, *Middlemarch*, the narrator

---

[46] *L* iii. 66.

[47] For Eliot's description of herself as 'morbid', see *L* iii. 321. For Ashton's account of the resemblance between Eliot and Latimer, see *George Eliot*, 220.

[48] *L* ii. 360.

hypothesizes that our sensitivity to the interior life of others is necessarily limited, for we could 'hardly bear' to have a full understanding of what they feel and think and suffer: 'If we had a keen vision and feeling of all ordinary human life, it would be like hearing the grass grow, and the squirrel's heart beat, and we should die of that roar which lies on the other side of silence.'[49] Latimer offers an altogether more cynical analysis: we should be loathe to see the poverty of our fellow creatures' souls. His language is at points strikingly anticipatory of *Middlemarch* (his clairvoyance was, he tells us, 'like a preternaturally heightened sense of hearing, making audible to one a roar of sound where others would find perfect stillness' (18)) but the moral pay-off is worlds apart: 'weariness', 'annoyance', and 'disgust'.

When Edith Simcox told G. H. Lewes that she could not help wanting a moral from 'The Lifted Veil', he supplied one with alacrity: 'Oh, but the moral is plain enough—it is only an exaggeration of what happens—the one-sided knowing of things in relation to the self—not whole knowledge because "tout comprehendre [*sic*] est tout pardonner" '.[50] Lewes was, in one sense, right: Latimer does not possess full knowledge, and his insight is a travesty of the ideal of such fullness. But the proverbial 'to know everything is to forgive everything' is Lewes's addition, based no doubt on familiarity with the moral beliefs Eliot had expressed elsewhere. Yet in 'The Lifted Veil' she had singularly refused to rearticulate them.

As it happened, Eliot had already provided the story with a moral of her own. In 1873 she turned down an opportunity to reprint the tale. 'I care for the idea which it embodies and which justifies its painfulness', she insisted: 'There are many things in it which I would willingly say over again, and I shall never put them in any other form. But we must wait a little. . . . [T]he best effect of writing . . . often depends on circumstances much as pictures depend on light and juxtaposition.'[51] With that letter to Blackwood she enclosed a newly composed motto for 'The Lifted Veil' which, she said, gave 'a sufficient indication' of the idea she had had in mind. It became, from the Cabinet Edition onwards, the story's epigraph:

---

[49] *Middlemarch: A Study of Provincial Life*, ed. David Carroll (Oxford: Oxford University Press, 1986), 189.

[50] *L* ix. 220.

[51] *L* v. 380.

> Give me no light, great Heaven, but such as turns
> To energy of human fellowship;
> No powers beyond the growing heritage
> That makes completer manhood.

It is a prayer to be spared exceptional acuity of the sort Latimer is compelled to endure at the cost of human fellowship and of a life worth the name. But it is also an attempt to close down the threat of what she had allowed herself to imagine. Fourteen years on, she was seeking to draw a positive ethical statement from her story which her younger self had declined; so the motto courts our compassionate insight into its narrator while he himself mocks us with the impossibility of sympathy.

John Blackwood sought to mute his own criticism of 'The Lifted Veil' on first reading it by conceding that 'others are not so fond of sweets as I'.[52] 'Brother Jacob'—the tale of a rogue confectioner—is just what he seems to have been looking for (though, as it happened, Eliot gave the story not to *Blackwood's* but to the *Cornhill Magazine*, to compensate the editor, George Smith, for the loss he had sustained on *Romola*). If 'The Lifted Veil' is the most sombre of all her works, 'Brother Jacob' is the most robustly comic. Though not originally conceived as a duo, they make a natural pairing as the only two self-contained short stories she produced: the *'jeux d'esprit'*, as Henry James put it (unknowingly echoing Eliot's *jeu de melancolie*) 'of a mind that is not often—perhaps not often enough—found at play'. That she did not experiment more extensively with the form may well be because these first efforts found few such warm admirers. Indeed, one of the reasons the stories came to be published together, with *Silas Marner*, in the prestigious 1878 Cabinet Edition of Eliot's works was her desire to protect 'The Lifted Veil' by giving it the right companion. 'Brother Jacob' was the perfect tonal contrast.

This witty fable is a sharp rebuke to a recurrent charge from Eliot's detractors that she had no sense of humour. It is a wonderfully irreverent portrait of a man who has not a shred of Eliot's moral sensibility about him—who steals his mother's guineas in order to pay his way to the West Indies where he hopes to find a princess

[52] *L* iii. 66.

gullible enough to be charmed by his bandy legs, sallow complexion, and timid green eyes and shower him with 'very large jewels . . . after which, he needn't marry her unless he liked' (57). Finding no one so desperate in the Indies, and no rewards just for being white, David Faux resumes his abandoned trade as a cook until he earns enough (with some additional income by the way of blackmail) to pay his way back to England. There, under the name of Edward Freely, he sets up a confectionery shop in the small rural town of Grimworth and proceeds to corrupt the domestic morals of the town's women-folk, gradually drawing them away from the time-honoured skills of home-cooking, to the improvement of their dinners but the impoverishment of their husbands' purses. He is well on the way to becoming a respected townsman, and to marrying pretty Penny Palfrey (whose father farms his own land and is, therefore, at the pinnacle of Grimworth society), when he meets his Nemesis in the person of his idiot brother Jacob, whose passion for guinea-like lozenges leads him to find out his 'sweet-tasting brother' and innocently expose him to the townsfolk.

'Brother Jacob' is more than tonally an antidote to 'The Lifted Veil''s sombreness. Many of the same elements recur: a resented brother, an oppressive father, a tender mother, foreign travel, the father's death, the pursuit of a blonde woman. But in place of the earlier tale's determined medical realism and its thwarted Rous-seauean Romanticism 'Brother Jacob' presents a satirical fable about a man whose literary tastes are much more towards the popular end of the scale: 'Inkle and Yarico' and cheap romances. In the *Spectator* for 13 March 1711, Richard Steele tells the story of a beautiful native American Indian woman, Yarico, who saves the life of a young London merchant, Thomas Inkle, only to be taken by him to Barbados and sold into slavery. When she pleads with him that she is carrying his child he heartlessly uses the information to drive up her sale price. There were numerous eighteenth-century adapta-tions of the story (itself an embroidered version of a tale from Richard Ligon's *A True and Exact History of the Island of Barbados*, 1657), among them George Colman Jr.'s musical play *Inkle and Yarico* (1787) performed successfully at Covent Garden and at the Haymarket. The point of David Faux's frequent reference to it is, of course, his gross misapplication of the moral, his knowledge of things in relation to the self being every bit as one-sided as Latimer's only without a hint of self-reflection. As a 'friend' of the narrator puts it, with (probably) a poor jab at quoting Virgil, this is a *'mens nil conscia sibi'*—literally, 'a mind not conscious of itself', more loosely, 'a mind without self-knowledge'.[53] But 'The Lifted Veil''s appalled recognition that psychological insight might be an insufficient guarantee for morality is here defused into comic acceptance that egotism and deception are the way of the world.

In one of the most substantial discussions of 'Brother Jacob' to date, Peter Allan Dale argues that Eliot took up from Lewes a critique of Bentham and Smith's view of the world that had its roots in the new physiology of mind. For the prophets of free enterprise man was a rational creature, calculating the most profitable way to secure his own interests in the world. For the physiologists that rationality was a surface. Man was at base an animal, 'motivated by subrational impulses or instincts that unite[d] him with the animals'—and idiots were a reminder of that union, showing (as a later nineteenth-century evolutionist would put it) 'a human mind arrested in its development, as well as deflected in its growth—therefore . . . supplying the comparative physiologist very suggestive material for study'.[54]

It is worth adding that in order to make this monitory use of the idiot brother Jacob Eliot was obliged to disregard the new humanitarian approach to idiocy celebrated by Dickens, amongst others, in *Household Words* and (later) *All the Year Round*.[55] At Dr Guggenbühl's much-praised mountain clinic in Switzerland a combination of moral management and education had produced remarkable advances in the capabilities of idiot children. Dr John Langdon Down's Idiot Asylum at Earlswood, Surrey, was established on similar principles in 1853, with more institutions rapidly following in other counties.[56] Such places gave rise to a great deal of optimism, not

[53] See Explanatory Notes, p. 98.

[54] George Romanes, *Mental Evolution in Animals* (London: Kegan Paul, 1885), 181, quoted in Peter Allan Dale, 'George Eliot's "Brother Jacob": Fables and the Physiology of Common Life', *Philological Quarterly*, 64/1 (1985), 17–35.

[55] See [Charles Dickens], 'Idiots', *Household Words*, 167 (4 June 1853), 313–17; [Harriet Martineau], 'Idiots Again', *Household Words*, 212 (15 Apr. 1854), 197–200; and [Andrew Halliday], 'Happy Idiots', *All the Year Round*, 274 (23 July 1864), 564–9 (on the Earlswood Asylum).

[56] See David Wright and Anne Digby (eds.), *From Idiocy to Mental Deficiency: Historical Perspectives on People with Learning Disabilities* (London: Routledge, 1996), 8.

always justified, on the part of social commentators, who saw Britain making rapid advances into a more humane age. Eliot's Jacob, however, marks a step back into the less enlightened past, and to the village idiot Dickens recalled as 'a thing of our childhood in an English country town':

a shambling knock-kneed man who was never a child, with an eager utterance of discordant sounds which he seemed to keep in his protruding forehead, with a tongue too large for his mouth, and a dreadful pair of hands that wanted to ramble over everything—our own face included.[57]

Jacob has the relative liberty of a 'village idiot' of the 1820s (when 'Brother Jacob' is set). No one checks him when he pursues David on his guinea-laden journey from home or, later, when he finds him out in Grimworth (though he is sought after a couple of days). Notwithstanding its progressiveness, writing about idiots in the 1860s often preserved some of the older motifs, particularly the traditional view of the idiot as a holy fool or innocent who unwittingly exposes the world's vices. Andrew Halliday's article for *All the Year Round* (July 1864), for example, describes a tour of the Earlswood Asylum on which he encounters an idiot remarkably like Jacob:

The lad who accompanied me told me he was a good farmer but a complete idiot. He could not count the pigs in a sty, though there were barely a dozen of them; but he was a most useful member of the establishment for all that. He spoke very imperfectly. I asked him if he were happy there. He said, 'Yes, very happy, but no money.' I asked him what he would do with money if he had any. He said 'Buy sweetstuff.' . . . They were all extremely fond of money, but the amount was of no consequence. They were just as pleased with a pound as a shilling.[58]

This is precisely Jacob's charm for the reader: he exactly replicates David's ravenous greed, but with no concept whatsoever of the value of enterprise, profit, or property. He thus provides a mirror image of David's selfishness, distorted into the cruder form of an insatiable appetite for food.

The redeeming feature in this relentlessly satiric tale of animal

---

[57] [Dickens], 'Idiots', 313.
[58] [Halliday], 'Happy Idiots', 567–8.

greed, Dale suggests, is that Eliot nevertheless places her faith in our power to connect imaginatively with our fellow beings through the rational deployment of symbols—that is, through art and literature. To this there is, of course, the reply that literature is almost entirely an instrument of self-promotion or self-protection in 'Brother Jacob': David abusively identifies himself with Inkle and uses second-hand verses to court the easily impressed, and even by his standards under-read, Penny Palfrey; above all, the narrator repeatedly indulges himself (the voice is ungendered, but implicitly masculine) in sardonic reference to a world of literature (Virgil, Shakespeare, Balzac) which unites him with the implied, cultivated reader, but at the expense of the people of Grimworth. Then again, comedy, especially in the satiric mode, is always its own get-out clause.

In principle, of course, there is no reason why 'Brother Jacob' should not be dealt with as seriously as 'The Lifted Veil'. Certainly it has discernible roots in Eliot's reading—including, once again, her familiarity with contemporary physiology. Lewes's *Physiology of Common Life* devotes a several-page section to 'Sugar', which, appropriately enough in view of David Faux's fickle character, demonstrates the remarkably 'plastic property' of the substance he works with. Lewes went on to pose the sobering questions 'Is sugar injurious to the teeth? Is it injurious to the stomach?'

To answer the first, we have only to point to the Negroes, who eat more sugar than any other human beings, and whose teeth are of enviable splendour and strength.

To answer the second is not so easy; yet, when we learn the important offices which sugar fulfils in the organism, we may be certain that, if injurious at all, it is only so in excess. The lactic acid formed from sugar dissolves phosphate of lime, and this, as we know, is the principal ingredient of bones and teeth. . . .

Timid parents may therefore check their alarm at the sight of juvenile forays on the sugar-basin when not excessive; may cease to vex children by forbidding moderate commercial transactions with the lolly-pop merchant, and cease to frustrate their desires for barley-sugar by the never-appreciated pretext, that the interdict is 'for their good'.[59]

Compare the narrator of 'Brother Jacob' reflecting on the popularity

[59] Lewes, *Physiology of Common Life*, 140, 141. For an alternative reading of 'Brother Jacob' alongside Lewes's work, see Dale, 'George Eliot's "Brother Jacob"', 17–35.

of Edward Freely's fancy-sugar department with the local schoolboys:

When I think of the sweet-tasted swans and other ingenious white shapes crunched by the small teeth of that rising generation, I am glad to remember that a certain amount of calcareous food has been held good for young creatures whose bones are not quite formed . . . (66)

There is a rather weightier philosophical point to be made in relation to the first page of 'Brother Jacob'. Eliot begins her fable with an elaborate philosophical meditation in defence of David Faux's too precipitate choice of a profession which delighted him as a child, but which as a no longer so sweet-toothed adult leaves him sadly wiser to the fact that confectioners do not hold a high place in society and have a very limited sphere in which to exercise their ambition. She continues:

I have known a man who turned out to have a metaphysical genius, incautiously, in the period of youthful buoyancy, commence his career as a dancing-master; and you may imagine the use that was made of this initial mistake by opponents who felt themselves bound to warn the public against his doctrine of the Inconceivable. (49)

It reads, perhaps, as a throwaway gesture (previous editors have left it unannotated), but it brings into view a complex debate within metaphysics which expanded the repercussions of her 'slight Tale'.[60] 'Brother Jacob' is a fable of the kind much more commonly employed in the Enlightenment, most famously by Johnson in *Rasselas* and Voltaire in *Candide*: a deceptively light vehicle for philosophical debate. The genre allows Eliot to put in play here, for those readers equipped to recognize it, a fundamental question about whether there are 'necessary truths' independent of our perception of them. In his *System of Logic* (1843), John Stuart Mill—the great leader of the 'empirical' as opposed to what he called the 'intuitional school' of philosophers—had taken issue with William Whewell's claim that 'Necessary truths are those in which . . . the negation of the truth is not only false, but impossible; in which we cannot, even by an effort of imagination, or in a supposition, conceive the reverse

[60] *J.* 86.

of that which is asserted.'[61] Mill responded, 'I cannot but wonder that so much stress should be laid upon the circumstance of inconceivableness, when there is such ample experience to show, that our capacity or incapacity of conceiving a thing has very little to do with the possibility of the thing in itself'.[62] For the Scottish philosopher Sir William Hamilton, however, truth was, finally, a question of morality. His views were stated most fully in his *Lectures on Metaphysics and Logic* (1859–60) where he set out his doctrine of the phenomenal and relative status of all knowledge, urging that we cannot have access to ultimate reality because knowledge is always coloured by the mind. If we attempt to do so we are left with what he called 'contradictory inconceivables'—the Absolute (that is, limited) on the one hand and the Infinite on the other. One of them, he asserted, must be true, and we therefore accept the alternative justified by our 'moral and religious feelings'.[63]

David Faux, alias Edward Freely, feels no such promptings, changing his name and rewriting his history as it suits his commercial and social ambitions, in the process avoiding unpleasant recriminations for past deeds. The only relevant criterion for David is how quickly he can convert sweets into guineas—until a necessary truth confronts him in the person of his idiot brother, Jacob. In terms of his actions David is in a moral category of his own at Grimworth, but he is not, perhaps, so isolated from his fellow townsfolk philosophically. Eliot makes affectionate play with just how far relativism is built into the moral life of her imaginary English town. One of the first things we learn about Grimworth is that it harbours, like so many nineteenth-century towns, a clear divide between Church and Chapel; that is, between those who attend the established Anglican church, and the 'Dissenters' (an umbrella term, including the Quakers, Independents (or Congregationalists), Baptists, Presbyterians and Unitarians, the many varieties of Methodism, and numerous smaller groupings). They have their separate grocers and their sep-

[61] William Whewell, *Philosophy of the Inductive Sciences* (London: John W. Parker, 1840), i. 54. The debate is reconstructed in greater detail in the Explanatory Notes, pp. 96–7.

[62] John Stuart Mill, *A System of Logic*, 2 vols. (London: John Parker & Son, 1843), i. 313.

[63] William Hamilton, *Lectures on Metaphysics and Logic* (Edinburgh: John Blackwood & Sons, 1859–60), 313.

arate drapers in Grimworth. But the butchers' shops indicate greater
flexibility when it suits, two or three of them enjoying the custom of
both groups—even if, as was usually the case, the Dissenters seem to
be lower down the social and economic pecking order: Mr Rodd, the
Baptist minister, has a standing order for cheap sheep's trotters,
whereas the rector's wife has first call on the pricier mutton kidneys
and veal sweetbreads.

This minor accommodation of principle to interest is replayed
time and again. The first Grimworth wife to lose the moral battle
against Freely's does so out of sheer desperation, having produced a
batch of mince pies which will never be acceptable to the rough
veterinary surgeon she has married. Once she has fallen, the slip is
easy for everyone else to make with the sure defence that '"other
people" did the same sort of thing' (65). With similar plasticity of
principle, the highest family in Grimworth—the Palfreys—will not
initially tolerate the admission of a mere confectioner to their home.
Yet judicious flattery of Mrs Palfrey's recipe for brawn, and the
invention of a rich and devoted uncle in the West Indies, soon
alter their minds. There is only one character who holds to 'necessary truths' in 'Brother Jacob'—and even for him they are less
Hamilton's moral truths than simple duties. David's other brother,
Jonathan, picks up the responsibility for feeding and nurturing Jacob
once their father dies, acknowledging the relationship immediately
he is asked where David has comically, and hopelessly, done his best
to throw it off: '"Ay, it's my innicent of a brother, sure enough," said
honest Jonathan. "A fine trouble and cost he is to us, in th'eating and
other things, but we must bear what's laid on us"' (84).

Although 'Brother Jacob' has not yet attracted anything like the
degree of critical attention given to 'The Lifted Veil' (and it is, for all
its wit, the slighter story), there has been interest in what this tale,
like the earlier one, has to say about George Eliot's sense of her role
as an artist.[64] As Susan de Sola Rodstein puts it, 'One could draw
many lines between Eliot and Faux, from leaving one's family and
remaking oneself to profiting from the sale of a luxury (novels) under

[64] See particularly Rosemarie Bodenheimer, *The Real Life of Mary Ann Evans: George
Eliot, Her Letters and Fiction* (Ithaca, NY: Cornell University Press, 1994), 148–51;
Ruby R. Redinger, *George Eliot: The Emergent Self* (London: Bodley Head, 1975), 435;
Susan de Sola Rodstein, 'Sweetness and Dark: George Eliot's "Brother Jacob"', *Modern
Language Quarterly*, 52/3 (1991), 295–317.

a new name.'[65] Several critics have wanted to read the story in the context of Eliot's dismay over the 'Liggins affair' of 1859, in which a Mr Joseph Liggins of Nuneaton, the son of a baker, and by some accounts a half-wit, became widely touted as the author of Eliot's *Scenes of Clerical Life*. If the narrator is to be believed, the great god Nemesis, and a fine peripeteia, await such deceivers. Yet, whereas the moral grafted on to 'The Lifted Veil' had tried to seal up the moral abyss of that story, 'Brother Jacob''s metaphor is a deliberate squib. David Faux heads out of Grimworth to start a new confectionery, no doubt, in another small country town with another sweet Penny Palfrey waiting to be courted. No one has been seriously corrupted by his influence: the matrons of Grimworth gradually revive their lapsed culinary skills, and even develop new heights of talent.

This, rather than 'The Lifted Veil', is Eliot's true *jeu d'esprit*. A spun-sugar creation, it begs for comparison with Thackeray's culinary masterpiece, *Pendennis*. Like that work, it makes extensive play with the time-honoured association between eating and reading, physical and imaginative consumption.[66] 'Knowledge is mental food,' Ruskin wrote, 'and is exactly to the spirit what food is to the body';[67] but as Thackeray more readily acknowledged, we do not require all our mental foods to be equally wholesome. 'I often say I am like the pastry cook,' he joked to Trollope in 1859: 'I don't care for tarts, but prefer bread and cheese; but the public love the tarts (luckily for us) and we must bake and sell them.'[68] It was a bonus for the Victorian reader that the best scientific authorities of the day were willing to testify that judicious indulgence in sweets was positively good for one's health.

[65] Rodstein, 'Sweetness and Dark', 315.

[66] Ruby Redinger suggests that the fable has a clear purport in relation to Eliot's contemporary literature: 'those publishers and reviewers who encouraged the production and consumption of saccharine literature which catered only to the taste of the public would be attacked by Jacob, who has no real need for the pitchfork because an idiot is . . . an "innocent"' (*George Eliot*, 435).

[67] John Ruskin, *The Stones of Venice* (1851–3), in E. T. Cook and Alexander Wedderburn (eds.), *The Complete Works of John Ruskin*, Library edn., 19 vols. (London: George Allen, 1903–12), xi. 63.

[68] Quoted in Anthony Trollope, *An Autobiography*, ed. David Skilton (London: Penguin Books, 1996), 91.

NOTE ON THE TEXT

'The Lifted Veil' was completed on 26 April 1859 and was first published in *Blackwood's Edinburgh Magazine* in July of that year. At John Blackwood's request it appeared anonymously, despite the recent success of *Adam Bede*, the 'better not to fritter away the prestige which should be kept fresh for the new novel [*The Mill on the Floss*]'. This edition reprints the text of the 1878 Cabinet Edition, corrected and revised by George Eliot. Most of the changes she made were slight, and evidently made for reasons of stylistic felicity (principally through lightening of punctuation, some substitutions of English words for French, and occasional modifications of word-choice). Extensive or particularly significant departures from the first printed text are recorded in the Explanatory Notes. One printer's error has been silently corrected.

'Brother Jacob' was composed in 1860 under the working title 'Mr David Faux, Confectioner'. With a revised title, 'The Idiot Boy', it was offered to the publishers Sampson Low for £250 but rejected. In February 1862 George Smith proposed to publish it in three parts in the *Cornhill Magazine* and suggested a payment of 250 guineas. The story was too short for part-publication, however, and publication was delayed until July 1864. In the event Eliot made a gift of the story to Smith, who had lost money on the publication of *Romola* (1862–3). 'Brother Jacob' appeared unsigned and accompanied by two illustrations—a frontispiece and initial letter drawing—designed by Charles Samuel Keene and engraved by Joseph Swain (reproduced on pp. 47 and 48 of this edition). The text printed is that of the Cabinet Edition corrected and very lightly revised by Eliot.

In two matters of punctuation Oxford house style has been imposed: single quotation marks have been used rather than double; and where a colon or semicolon follows direct speech or a quotation it has been placed outside rather than inside the closing quotation mark.

SELECT BIBLIOGRAPHY

Primary Material and Biographies

Rosemary Ashton, *George Eliot: A Life* (London: Hamish Hamilton, 1996).

George Eliot, *The George Eliot Letters*, ed. Gordon S. Haight, 9 vols. (New Haven: Yale University Press, 1954–78).

—— *The Journals of George Eliot*, ed. Margaret Harris and Judith Johnston (Cambridge: Cambridge University Press, 1998).

—— *Essays of George Eliot*, ed. Thomas Pinney (New York: New York University Press, 1963).

Gordon Haight, *George Eliot: A Biography* (Oxford: Clarendon Press, 1968)—the standard biography.

Critical Studies of Both Stories

Kristin Brady, *George Eliot*, Macmillan Women Writers series (London: Macmillan, 1992).

Henry James, '"The Lifted Veil" and "Brother Jacob"', *Nation*, 26 (25 Apr. 1878), 277; rpt. in Gordon S. Haight (ed.), *A Century of George Eliot Criticism* (Boston: Houghton Mifflin, 1965).

U. C. Knoepflmacher, *George Eliot's Early Novels: The Limits of Realism* (Berkeley: University of California Press, 1968).

Ruby R. Redinger, *George Eliot: The Emergent Self* (London: The Bodley Head, 1975).

Sally Shuttleworth, *George Eliot and Nineteenth-Century Science: The Make-Believe of a Beginning* (Cambridge: Cambridge University Press, 1984).

Jenny Uglow, *George Eliot* (London: Virago, 1987).

Alexander Welsh, *George Eliot and Blackmail* (Cambridge, Mass.: Harvard University Press, 1985).

'The Lifted Veil'

Gillian Beer, 'Myth and the Single Consciousness: *Middlemarch* and *The Lifted Veil*', in Ian Adam (ed.), *This Particular Web: Essays on 'Middlemarch'* (Toronto: University of Toronto Press, 1975), 91–115.

Malcolm Bull, 'Mastery and Slavery in *The Lifted Veil*', *Essays in Criticism*, 48 (1998), 244–61.

David Carroll, *George Eliot and the Conflict of Interpretations: A Reading of the Novels* (Cambridge: Cambridge University Press, 1992).

Terry Eagleton, 'Power and Knowledge in "The Lifted Veil"', *Literature and History*, 9/1 (1983), 52–61.

Kate Flint, 'Blood, Bodies, and *The Lifted Veil*', *Nineteenth-Century Literature*, 51/4 (1997), 455–73.

Richard Freedman, *Eliot, James and the Fictional Self: A Study in Character and Narrative* (London: Macmillan, 1986).

Sandra M. Gilbert and Susan Gubar, *The Madwoman in the Attic: The Woman Writer and the Nineteenth-Century Literary Imagination* (New Haven: Yale University Press, 1979).

B. M. Gray, 'Pseudoscience and George Eliot's "The Lifted Veil"', *Nineteenth-Century Fiction*, 36/4 (1982), 407–23.

—— Afterword to *The Lifted Veil* (London: Virago, 1985).

—— Afterword to *Brother Jacob* (London: Virago, 1989).

Graham Handley, '"The Lifted Veil" and its Relation to George Eliot's Fiction', *The George Eliot Fellowship Review*, 15 (1984), 64–9.

Mary Jacobus, *Reading Woman: Essays in Feminist Criticism* (New York: Columbia University Press, 1986).

Judith Siford, '"Dismal Loneliness": George Eliot, Auguste Comte and "The Lifted Veil"', *The George Eliot Review*, 26 (1995), 46–52.

Charles Swann, 'Déjà Vu: Déjà Lu: "The Lifted Veil" as an Experiment in Art', *Literature and History*, 5/1 (1979), 40–57, 86.

Marcia M. Taylor, 'Born Again: Reviving Bertha Grant', *George Eliot George Henry Lewes Newsletter*, 18–19 (1991), 46–54.

Carroll Viera, '"The Lifted Veil" and George Eliot's Early Aesthetic', *Studies in English Literature*, 24 (1984), 749–67.

Anne D. Wallace, '"Vague Capricious Memories": *The Lifted Veil*'s Challenge to Wordsworthian Poetics', *George Eliot George Henry Lewes Newsletter*, 18–19 (1991), 31–45.

Judith Wilt, *Ghosts of the Gothic: Austen, Eliot, and Lawrence* (Princeton: Princeton University Press, 1980).

Hugh Witemeyer, 'George Eliot and Jean-Jacques Rousseau', *Comparative Literature Studies*, 16/2 (1979), 121–30.

Jane Wood, 'Scientific Rationality and Fanciful Fiction: Gendered Discourse in *The Lifted Veil*', *Women's Writing*, 3/2 (1996), 161–76.

'Brother Jacob'

Rosemarie Bodenheimer, *The Real Life of Mary Ann Evans: George Eliot, Her Letters and Fiction* (Ithaca, NY: Cornell University Press, 1994).

Peter Allan Dale, 'George Eliot's "Brother Jacob": Fables and the

Physiology of Common Life', *Philological Quarterly*, 64/1 (1985), 17–35.

Susan de Sola Rodstein, 'Sweetness and Dark: George Eliot's "Brother Jacob"', *Modern Language Quarterly*, 52/3 (1991), 295–317.

Further Reading in Oxford World's Classics

George Eliot, *Adam Bede*, ed. Valentine Cunningham.

—— *Daniel Deronda*, ed. Graham Handley.

—— *Felix Holt, the Radical*, ed. Fred C. Thomson.

—— *Middlemarch*, ed. David Carroll, with an introduction by Felicia Bonaparte.

—— *The Mill on the Floss*, ed. Gordon S. Haight, with an introduction by Dinah Birch.

—— *Scenes of Clerical Life*, ed. Thomas A. Noble.

—— *Silas Marner*, ed. Terence Cave.

A CHRONOLOGY OF GEORGE ELIOT

	Life	*Cultural and Historical Background*
1819	Born, 22 November, at South Farm, Arbury, nr Nuneaton, Warwickshire, the youngest of the 3 children of Robert Evans and his second wife Christiana Pearson. Christened Mary Ann Evans, 29 November	Birth of Victoria. Scott, *The Bride of Lammermoor*, *Ivanhoe*
1820	Evans family moves to Griff House, Arbury, where Robert Evans is agent for Francis Newdigate's estate	Death of George III; accession of George IV. Keats, *Lamia, . . . and other Poems*; Shelley, *Prometheus Unbound*
1824–7	Boarder at Miss Lathom's School in nearby Attleborough, with her sister Chrissey	
1828–32	At Mrs Wallington's boarding-school, Nuneaton, where she becomes friendly with Miss Lewis, the principal governess and a strong evangelical	1829: Catholic Emancipation Act 1830: Death of George IV; accession of William IV. Tennyson, *Poems, Chiefly Lyrical* 1830–3: Charles Lyell, *Principles of Geology*
1832–5	At the Misses Franklin's School, Coventry, run by the daughters of a Baptist minister. Leaves school finally at Christmas	1832: First Reform Act 1833: First Factory Act 1835: David Friedrich Strauss, *Das Leben Jesu*
1836	Mother dies 3 February. After Chrissey marries, in May 1837, GE takes charge of her father's household. Learns Italian and Greek from a Coventry teacher, and reads Greek and Latin with the headmaster of Coventry Grammar School	
1837–9	Reads widely, especially in theology, the history of religion, and in Romanticism, including Wordsworth, Coleridge, Southey, and Scott (her favourite novelist)	1837: Death of William IV; accession of Victoria. Carlyle, *The French Revolution*; Dickens, *Pickwick Papers* 1838: Anti Corn Law League founded; London–Birmingham railway opened

		1839: Chartists demand suffrage; Charles Hennell, *An Inquiry into the Origins of Christianity*
1840	Her first publication, a religious poem, appears in the *Christian Observer* in January	Penny Post established; Victoria marries Prince Albert
1841	Brother, Isaac, marries and takes over the house at Griff. GE moves with father to Coventry. Introduced to Charles Bray and his wife Caroline (Cara), Coventry free-thinkers, through whom she makes contact with Charles Hennell. Reads Hennell's *Inquiry* and finds her religious faith challenged	Robert Peel becomes Prime Minister. Carlyle, *Heroes and Hero Worship*
1842	Refuses to attend church with her father, January–May, but finally agrees to accompany him at the end of what she calls their 'Holy War'. Meets and begins corresponding with Charles Hennell's sister Sara	Chartist riots; child and female underground labour becomes illegal; Act for inspection of asylums. Browning, *Dramatic Lyrics*; Comte, *Cours de philosophie positive*; Macaulay, *Lays of Ancient Rome*; Tennyson, *Poems*
1843	In November visits Dr Brabant of Devizes, father of Charles Hennell's wife who had undertaken a translation of Strauss's *Das Leben Jesu* but, on marrying, discontinued it	Thames Tunnel opened. Carlyle, *Past and Present*; Ruskin, *Modern Painters* begins publication; Wordsworth, *Poems*
1844	Takes over the translation of *Das Leben Jesu*	Robert Chambers's *Vestiges of Creation* published anonymously
1845	In March declines a proposal of marriage. Meets Harriet Martineau. In October visits Scotland with the Brays, and visits Scott's home, Abbotsford	Newman received into the Catholic Church; Irish potato crop fails. Disraeli, *Sybil; or, The Two Nations*
1846	*The Life of Jesus* published in 3 vols. in June after much labour and many complaints of being 'Strauss-sick'	Repeal of the Corn Laws; Irish famine. Ruskin, *Modern Painters* II
1847	Nurses her father	James Simpson discovers the anaesthetic properties of chloroform. 'Currer Bell', *Jane Eyre*; 'Ellis Bell', *Wuthering Heights*; Thackeray, *Vanity Fair*; Dickens, *Dombey and Son*

1848	Meets Emerson; reads Sand and Scott. Nurses her father	Revolutions in Europe; Disraeli becomes leader of the Tory party in the House of Commons. Elizabeth Gaskell, *Mary Barton*
1849	Reviews J. A. Froude's *Nemesis of Faith* favourably for the *Coventry Herald*. Begins translation of Spinoza's *Tractatus theologico-politicus*. Father dies on 31 May. In June leaves for France, Italy, and Switzerland with the Brays; winters alone in Geneva. Begins *Journal*	Cholera epidemic in England; Bedford College for Women founded. Henry Mayhew's 'London Labour and the London Poor' articles begin publication in the *Morning Chronicle*
1850	Returns, unhappily, to Coventry and lives with the Brays for seven months. Adopts the French spelling of her name, Marian, in preference to Mary Ann. Decides to earn her living by writing. Reviews Mackay's *The Progress of the Intellect* for the January no. of John Chapman's *Westminster Review* and lodges with him in London for two weeks in November	Death of Wordsworth. *The Prelude* published posthumously; Spencer, *Social Statics*; Dickens, *David Copperfield*
1851	Moves to John Chapman's home, 142 Strand, in January but in March is driven away by the jealousy of his wife and mistress. Returns in September to become, in all but name, the editor of the *Westminster Review*	Great Exhibition opens at the Crystal Palace
1852	Friendship with Herbert Spencer leads to rumours of an engagement. Through him she meets George Henry Lewes, arts editor of the *Leader*	Death of the Duke of Wellington, 14 September; Kings Cross station completed
1853	Heavily involved with the *Westminster Review*. Reads Gaskell's *Ruth*, Brontë's *Villette*, Goethe, Schiller, Lessing, and Hegel	Harriet Martineau's translation of Comte's *Positive Philosophy*; Dickens, *Bleak House*; Charlotte Brontë, *Villette*; Elizabeth Gaskell, *Ruth* and *Cranford*

1854	Her translation of Ludwig Feuerbach's radical critique of orthodox belief, *The Essence of Christianity* is published in July. In the same month she travels to Germany with Lewes, first visiting Weimar then wintering in Berlin, causing scandal back in Britain. Lewes unable to obtain a divorce because he had condoned his wife's adultery. Assists Lewes in the research and writing of his biography of Goethe and in November begins a translation of Spinoza's *Ethics* (unpublished until 1981)	Crimean War begins
1855	Returns to England in March and sets up house with Lewes in Richmond. Writes regularly for the *Leader* and *Westminster Review*. In November Lewes's *Life and Works of Goethe* is published to general and lasting acclaim	Gaskell, *North and South*; Turgenev, *Russian Life*, trans. James D. Meiklejohn
1856	Visits Ilfracombe, May–June, for Lewes's research into marine biology (later published as *Seaside Studies*, 1858), then Tenby in Wales, late June–July where begins writing 'The Sad Fortunes of the Rev. Amos Barton'. The story is accepted by *Blackwood's Edinburgh Magazine*. Her review of Riehl's *The Natural History of German Life* appears in the *Westminster Review* in July, and 'Silly Novels by Lady Novelists' in October	Crimean War ends 29 April; public celebrations of the peace with Russia are held across Britain on 29 May. Meredith, *The Shaving of Shagpat*

1857 In January Part 1 of 'Amos Barton' appears in *Blackwood's* and her last major article in the *Westminster Review*. Assumes the pseudonym 'George Eliot'. In March travels with Lewes to Scilly Isles where she writes 'Mr Gilfil's Love-Story' for the June issue of *Blackwood's*. Tells her family about her relationship and they break off all communication with her. 'Janet's Repentance' finished 30 May on Jersey, where they stay until late July. Begins writing *Adam Bede* in October

Indian Mutiny. Flaubert, *Madame Bovary*; Gaskell, *The Life of Charlotte Brontë*; Dickens, *Little Dorrit*

1858 *Scenes of Clerical Life* published in 2 vols. in January. Dickens writes praising the book, and convinced the author must be a woman. In April GE and Lewes travel via Nuremburg to Munich, remaining there until 6 July when they make their way via Salzburg, Vienna, and Prague to Dresden. Work on *Adam Bede* proceeds quickly. They return to England in September, and the novel is completed on 16 November

Government of India Act transferring British power over India from the East India Co. to the Crown; Burton and Speke discover source of the Nile; Bessie Parkes and Barbara Bodichon found the *English Woman's Journal* which campaigns for married women's property rights and higher education for women

1859 *Adam Bede* published in 3 vols. in February to critical acclaim; 16,000 copies sold in the first year. In February they settle at Holly Lodge, Wandsworth, where GE forms a close friendship with the positivists, Mr and Mrs Richard Congreve. Sister Chrissey dies of consumption in March. Work on *The Mill on the Floss* is slow, and she breaks off to write 'The Lifted Veil' (finished in April and published in *Blackwood's* in July). In June, under pressure, the secrecy of the pseudonym is relinquished. Dickens visits in November and invites her to contribute to *All the Year Round*

Charles Darwin, *The Origin of Species*; J. S. Mill, *On Liberty*; Tennyson, *Idylls of the King*; *Macmillan's Magazine* launched in November

1860	*The Mill on the Floss* finished on 22 March and published in 3 vols. on 4 April. GE and Lewes leave for a holiday in Italy where, in May, GE conceives the idea for a historical novel based on the life of Savonarola. They return to England via Switzerland, bringing Lewes's eldest son Charles back with them. GE abandons the Savonarola project in September in despair. Writes 'Brother Jacob'; begins *Silas Marner*. With Charles they move house twice, settling in December at 16 Blandford Square, off Regent's Park	Unification of Italy. *Cornhill Magazine* founded
1861	*Silas Marner* published in April; they revisit Florence where GE collects more material, and she begins writing *Romola* in October	American Civil War begins
1862	Smith, Elder offer the unprecedented sum of £10,000 for *Romola* (GE eventually accepts £7,000) which begins serialization in the *Cornhill Magazine* in July. As part of her research for the book reads Elizabeth Barrett Browning's *Casa Guidi Windows*	
1863	*Romola* published in 3 vols. in July and finishes serialization in the *Cornhill* in August: 'I began it as a young woman,—I finished it an old woman.' In August they move to the Priory, Regent's Park, the house associated with GE's most famous years	Thackeray dies suddenly on Christmas Eve; over 1,000 people attend the funeral. Elizabeth Gaskell, *Sylvia's Lovers*
1864	They visit Italy in May. In June GE begins research for *The Spanish Gypsy*, a tragic play in blank verse. Starts writing in October. Reading includes Newman's *Apologia pro Vita Sua*	Dickens, *Our Mutual Friend* begins publication

1865	Work on *The Spanish Gypsy* proves so stressful that Lewes insists she abandon it in February. Begins *Felix Holt* in March. Lewes becomes editor of the *Fortnightly Review* and GE contributes a review of Lecky	Abraham Lincoln assassinated, 14 April; American Civil War ends in May; death of Palmerston in October; Russell succeeds him as leader of the House of Commons. *Fortnightly Review* founded; Walter Bagehot's *The English Constitution* serialized; Lecky, *History of . . . Rationalism in Europe*
1866	*Felix Holt* completed in May and published in 3 vols. in June but sales disappoint. They visit the Low Countries and Germany, and in August GE resumes work on *The Spanish Gypsy*. In December they set off for the South of France	Russell's 1st Reform Bill defeated; in April Gladstone tells the House: 'You cannot fight against the future. Time is on our side'; rioting in Hyde Park on 23 July after the resignation of Russell's ministry; Austria and Prussia at war
1867	In January they extend their trip to Spain so that GE can collect material. On 22 February they visit gipsies living in holes in the mountains above Granada. Return on 16 March	2nd Reform Bill introduced by Disraeli; 20 May John Stuart Mill moves to amend the new Reform Bill to include women. Turgenev, *Fathers and Sons*, trans. E. Schuyler
1868	Gives £50 'from the author of *Romola*' to the foundation of what became Girton College, Cambridge. *The Spanish Gypsy* finished 29 April and published in June	Browning, *The Ring and the Book* begins publication
1869	Writes some short poems early in the year. March and April in Italy. In Rome GE meets the stockbroker John Walter Cross for the first time. Henry James visits in May. GE intermittently researches a long poem to be called 'Timoleon', but abandons the project in September. Begins writing 'Middlemarch' (the Featherstone–Vincy part) in August. Lewes's second son, Thornton (Thornie), returns from Natal in May with spinal tuberculosis and dies in October. GE writes the poems eventually published as *The Legend of Jubal and Other Poems* (1874)	Hitchin College opens in May (becomes Girton College in 1873). J. S. Mill, *The Subjection of Women*

1870	Puts aside 'Middlemarch' in despair, and in November begins a new story, 'Miss Brooke', which develops rapidly. Corresponds with Harriet Beecher Stowe. Combines the two narratives early in the year to create the first section of *Middlemarch*, to be published in 8 parts. Book I published in December	Franco-Prussian War begins; death of Dickens; Married Women's Property Act; Elementary Education Act
1871	Final part of *Middlemarch* published in December; the whole published in 4 vols.	Franco-Prussian War ends
1872	'Simmering towards a new book', November	Le Fanu, *In a Glass Darkly*
1873	Begins 'Sketches towards Daniel Deronda', January. July–August visits France and Germany to research the novel. *The Legend of Jubal and Other Poems* published	Pater, *Studies in the History of the Renaissance*
1874	*Poems* published, including the 'Brother and Sister sonnets'. Suffers a first attack of kidney stone in February. Begins writing *Daniel Deronda* in the late autumn, but progress is slow due to ill health. Vol. I of Lewes's *Problems of Life and Mind* published in November	Disraeli becomes Prime Minister. Hardy, *Far from the Madding Crowd*
1875	Writing *Daniel Deronda*. Vol. II of Lewes's *Problems of Life and Mind* published	Death of Kingsley. Trollope, *The Way We Live Now*
1876	*Daniel Deronda* begins publication in 8 parts in February, the last part appearing in September. Richard Wagner and his wife visit in May. June–September travelling in France, Germany, Switzerland. In December they buy The Heights at Witley in Surrey as a summer residence	Alexander Graham Bell patents the telephone. James, *Roderick Hudson*

1878	Writes *Impressions of Theophrastus Such*. Lewes dies on 30 November. GE refuses to see anyone for several weeks and occupies herself in completing and preparing the last two volumes of his major philosophical work, *Problems of Life and Mind*, for the press	London University becomes the first to offer degrees to women. Gilbert and Sullivan, *HMS Pinafore*
1879	Agrees to see Cross in February, and helps him to learn Italian. *Impressions of Theophrastus Such* published in June. Gives £5,000 to fund a Studentship in Physiology at Cambridge in Lewes's name, the first Student being appointed in October. For legal reasons changes her name by deed poll to Mary Ann Evans Lewes	Ibsen, *A Doll's House*; James, *Daisy Miller*
1880	In April agrees to marry Cross. Married on 6 May, upon which her brother Isaac writes to congratulate her after 23 years of estrangement. Honeymoons in France and Italy, principally Venice, returning to England via Austria and Germany in late July. Moves to 4 Cheyne Walk on 3 December. Catches cold at a concert and dies on 22 December aged 61, her death probably in part the result of kidney disease. Buried in Highgate Cemetery on 29 December	Elementary education becomes compulsory in England and Wales; Parnell demands Home Rule for Ireland. Tennyson, *Ballads and Other Poems*; Gissing, *Workers in the Dawn*

THE LIFTED VEIL*

Give me no light, great Heaven, but such as turns
To energy of human fellowship;
No powers beyond the growing heritage
That makes completer manhood.*

CHAPTER I

THE time of my end approaches. I have lately been subject to attacks of *angina pectoris;** and in the ordinary course of things, my physician tells me, I may fairly hope that my life will not be protracted many months. Unless, then, I am cursed with an exceptional physical constitution, as I am cursed with an exceptional mental character, I shall not much longer groan under the wearisome burthen of this earthly existence. If it were to be otherwise—if I were to live on to the age most men desire and provide for—I should for once have known whether the miseries of delusive expectation can outweigh the miseries of true prevision. For I foresee when I shall die, and everything that will happen in my last moments.

Just a month from this day, on the 20th of September 1850, I shall be sitting in this chair, in this study, at ten o'clock at night, longing to die, weary of incessant insight and foresight, without delusions and without hope. Just as I am watching a tongue of blue flame rising in the fire, and my lamp is burning low, the horrible contraction will begin at my chest. I shall only have time to reach the bell, and pull it violently, before the sense of suffocation will come. No one will answer my bell. I know why. My two servants are lovers, and will have quarrelled. My housekeeper will have rushed out of the house in a fury, two hours before, hoping that Perry will believe she has gone to drown herself. Perry is alarmed at last, and is gone out after her. The little scullery-maid is asleep on a bench: she never answers the bell; it does not wake her. The sense of suffocation increases: my lamp goes out with a horrible stench: I make a great effort, and snatch at the bell again. I long for life, and there is no help. I thirsted for the unknown: the thirst is gone. O God, let me stay with the known, and be weary of it: I am content. Agony of pain and suffocation—and all the while the earth, the fields, the pebbly brook at the bottom of the rookery, the fresh scent after the rain, the light of the morning through my chamber-window, the warmth of the hearth after the frosty air—will darkness close over them for ever?

Darkness—darkness—no pain—nothing but darkness: but I am passing on and on through the darkness: my thought stays in the darkness, but always with a sense of moving onward. . . .

Before that time comes, I wish to use my last hours of ease and strength in telling the strange story of my experience. I have never fully unbosomed myself to any human being; I have never been encouraged to trust much in the sympathy of my fellow-men. But we have all a chance of meeting with some pity, some tenderness, some charity, when we are dead: it is the living only who cannot be forgiven—the living only from whom men's indulgence and reverence are held off, like the rain by the hard east wind. While the heart beats, bruise it—it is your only opportunity; while the eye can still turn towards you with moist timid entreaty, freeze it with an icy unanswering gaze; while the ear, that delicate messenger to the inmost sanctuary of the soul, can still take in the tones of kindness, put it off with hard civility, or sneering compliment, or envious affectation of indifference; while the creative brain can still throb with the sense of injustice, with the yearning for brotherly recognition—make haste—oppress it with your ill-considered judgments, your trivial comparisons, your careless misrepresentations. The heart will by-and-by be still—*ubi sæva indignatio ulterius cor lacerare nequit;*[1]* the eye will cease to entreat; the ear will be deaf; the brain will have ceased from all wants as well as from all work. Then your charitable speeches may find vent; then you may remember and pity the toil and the struggle and the failure; then you may give due honour to the work achieved; then you may find extenuation for errors, and may consent to bury them.

That is a trivial schoolboy text; why do I dwell on it? It has little reference to me, for I shall leave no works behind me for men to honour. I have no near relatives who will make up, by weeping over my grave, for the wounds they inflicted on me when I was among them. It is only the story of my life that will perhaps win a little more sympathy from strangers when I am dead, than I ever believed it would obtain from my friends while I was living.

My childhood perhaps seems happier to me than it really was, by contrast with all the after-years. For then the curtain of the future was as impenetrable to me as to other children: I had all their delight in the present hour, their sweet indefinite hopes for the morrow; and I had a tender mother: even now, after the dreary lapse of long years, a slight trace of sensation accompanies the remembrance of her

---

[1] Inscription on Swift's tombstone.

caress as she held me on her knee—her arms round my little body, her cheek pressed on mine. I had a complaint of the eyes that made me blind for a little while, and she kept me on her knee from morning till night. That unequalled love soon vanished out of my life, and even to my childish consciousness it was as if that life had become more chill. I rode my little white pony with the groom by my side as before, but there were no loving eyes looking at me as I mounted, no glad arms opened to me when I came back. Perhaps I missed my mother's love more than most children of seven or eight would have done, to whom the other pleasures of life remained as before; for I was certainly a very sensitive child. I remember still the mingled trepidation and delicious excitement with which I was affected by the tramping of the horses on the pavement in the echoing stables, by the loud resonance of the grooms' voices, by the booming bark of the dogs as my father's carriage thundered under the archway of the courtyard, by the din of the gong as it gave notice of luncheon and dinner. The measured tramp of soldiery which I sometimes heard—for my father's house lay near a county town where there were large barracks—made me sob and tremble; and yet when they were gone past, I longed for them to come back again.

I fancy my father thought me an odd child, and had little fondness for me; though he was very careful in fulfilling what he regarded as a parent's duties. But he was already past the middle of life, and I was not his only son. My mother had been his second wife, and he was five-and-forty when he married her. He was a firm, unbending, intensely orderly man, in root and stem a banker, but with a flourishing graft of the active landholder, aspiring to county influence: one of those people who are always like themselves from day to day, who are uninfluenced by the weather, and neither know melancholy nor high spirits. I held him in great awe, and appeared more timid and sensitive in his presence than at other times; a circumstance which, perhaps, helped to confirm him in the intention to educate me on a different plan from the prescriptive one with which he had complied in the case of my elder brother, already a tall youth at Eton. My brother was to be his representative and successor; he must go to Eton and Oxford, for the sake of making connections, of course: my father was not a man to underrate the bearing of Latin satirists or Greek dramatists on the attainment of an aristocratic position. But, intrinsically, he had slight esteem for 'those dead but sceptred

spirits';* having qualified himself for forming an independent
opinion by reading Potter's 'Æschylus', and dipping into Francis's
'Horace'.* To this negative view he added a positive one, derived
from a recent connection with mining speculations;* namely, that a
scientific education was the really useful training for a younger son.
Moreover, it was clear that a shy, sensitive boy like me was not fit to
encounter the rough experience of a public school. Mr Letherall*
had said so very decidedly. Mr Letherall was a large man in
spectacles, who one day took my small head between his large hands,
and pressed it here and there in an exploratory, suspicious manner—
then placed each of his great thumbs on my temples, and pushed me
a little way from him, and stared at me with glittering spectacles.
The contemplation appeared to displease him, for he frowned
sternly, and said to my father, drawing his thumbs across my
eyebrows—

'The deficiency is there, sir—there; and here,' he added, touching
the upper sides of my head, 'here is the excess. That must be brought
out, sir, and this must be laid to sleep.'

I was in a state of tremor, partly at the vague idea that I was the
object of reprobation, partly in the agitation of my first hatred—
hatred of this big, spectacled man, who pulled my head about as if he
wanted to buy and cheapen it.

I am not aware how much Mr Letherall had to do with the system
afterwards adopted towards me, but it was presently clear that private tutors, natural history, science, and the modern languages, were
the appliances by which the defects of my organisation were to be
remedied. I was very stupid about machines, so I was to be greatly
occupied with them; I had no memory for classification, so it was
particular necessary that I should study systematic zoology and botany; I was hungry for human deeds and human emotions, so I was to
be plentifully crammed with the mechanical powers, the elementary
bodies, and the phenomena of electricity and magnetism. A better-
constituted boy would certainly have profited under my intelligent
tutors, with their scientific apparatus; and would, doubtless, have
found the phenomena of electricity and magnetism as fascinating as I
was, every Thursday, assured they were. As it was, I could have paired
off, for ignorance of whatever was taught me, with the worst Latin
scholar that was ever turned out of a classical academy.* I read
Plutarch,* and Shakespeare, and Don Quixote by the sly, and supplied

myself in that way with wandering thoughts, while my tutor was assuring me that 'an improved man, as distinguished from an ignorant one, was a man who knew the reason why water ran down-hill.' I had no desire to be this improved man; I was glad of the running water; I could watch it and listen to it gurgling among the pebbles, and bathing the bright green water-plants, by the hour together. I did not want to know *why* it ran; I had perfect confidence that there were good reasons for what was so very beautiful.

There is no need to dwell on this part of my life. I have said enough to indicate that my nature was of the sensitive, unpractical order, and that it grew up in an uncongenial medium, which could never foster it into happy, healthy development. When I was sixteen I was sent to Geneva* to complete my course of education; and the change was a very happy one to me, for the first sight of the Alps, with the setting sun on them, as we descended the Jura, seemed to me like an entrance into heaven; and the three years of my life there were spent in a perpetual sense of exaltation, as if from a draught of delicious wine, at the presence of Nature in all her awful loveliness. You will think, perhaps, that I must have been a poet, from this early sensibility to Nature. But my lot was not so happy as that. A poet pours forth his song and *believes* in the listening ear and answering soul, to which his song will be floated sooner or later. But the poet's sensibility without his voice—the poet's sensibility that finds no vent but in silent tears on the sunny bank, when the noonday light sparkles on the water, or in an inward shudder at the sound of harsh human tones, the sight of a cold human eye—this dumb passion brings with it a fatal solitude of soul in the society of one's fellow-men. My least solitary moments were those in which I pushed off in my boat, at evening, towards the centre of the lake; it seemed to me that the sky, and the glowing mountain-tops, and the wide blue water, surrounded me with a cherishing love such as no human face had shed on me since my mother's love had vanished out of my life. I used to do as Jean Jacques* did—lie down in my boat and let it glide where it would, while I looked up at the departing glow leaving one mountain-top after the other, as if the prophet's chariot of fire* were passing over them on its way to the home of light. Then, when the white summits were all sad and corpse-like, I had to push homeward, for I was under careful surveillance, and was allowed no late wanderings. This disposition of mine was not favourable to the formation of intimate friendships among the numerous youths of my own age who are always to be found studying at Geneva. Yet I made *one* such friendship; and, singularly enough, it was with a youth whose intellectual tendencies were the very reverse of my own. I shall call him Charles Meunier;* his real surname—an English one, for he was of English extraction—having since become celebrated. He was an orphan, who lived on a miserable pittance while he pursued the medical studies for which he had a special genius. Strange! that with my vague mind, susceptible and unobservant, hating inquiry and given up to contemplation, I should have been drawn towards a youth whose strongest passion was science. But the bond was not an intellectual one; it came from a source that can happily blend the stupid with the brilliant, the dreamy with the practical: it came from community of feeling. Charles was poor and ugly, derided by Genevese *gamins*,* and not acceptable in drawing-rooms. I saw that he was isolated, as I was, though from a different cause, and, stimulated by a sympathetic resentment, I made timid advances towards him. It is enough to say that there sprang up as much comradeship between us as our different habits would allow; and in Charles's rare holidays we went up the Salève together, or took the boat to Vevay,* while I listened dreamily to the monologues in which he unfolded his bold conceptions of future experiment and discovery. I mingled them confusedly in my thought with glimpses of blue water and delicate floating cloud, with the notes of birds and the distant glitter of the glacier. He knew quite well that my mind was half absent, yet he liked to talk to me in this way; for don't we talk of our hopes and our projects even to dogs and birds, when they love us? I have mentioned this one friendship because of its connection with a strange and terrible scene which I shall have to narrate in my subsequent life.

This happier life at Geneva was put an end to by a severe illness, which is partly a blank to me, partly a time of dimly-remembered suffering, with the presence of my father by my bed from time to time. Then came the languid monotony of convalescence, the days gradually breaking into variety and distinctness as my strength enabled me to take longer and longer drives. On one of these more vividly remembered days, my father said to me, as he sat beside my sofa—

'When you are quite well enough to travel, Latimer, I shall take you home with me. The journey will amuse you and do you good, for

I shall go through the Tyrol and Austria, and you will see many new places. Our neighbours, the Filmores, are come; Alfred will join us at Basle, and we shall all go together to Vienna, and back by Prague'*...

My father was called away before he had finished his sentence, and he left my mind resting on the word *Prague*, with a strange sense that a new and wondrous scene was breaking upon me: a city under the broad sunshine, that seemed to me as if it were the summer sunshine of a long-past century arrested in its course—unrefreshed for ages by the dews of night, or the rushing rain-cloud; scorching the dusty, weary, time-eaten grandeur of a people doomed to live on in the stale repetition of memories, like deposed and superannuated kings, in their regal gold-inwoven tatters. The city looked so thirsty that the broad river seemed to me a sheet of metal; and the blackened statues, as I passed under their blank gaze, along the unending bridge,* with their ancient garments and their saintly crowns, seemed to me the real inhabitants and owners of this place, while the busy, trivial men and women, hurrying to and fro, were a swarm of ephemeral visit-ants infesting it for a day. It is such grim, stony beings as these, I thought, who are the fathers of ancient faded children, in those tanned time-fretted dwellings that crowd the steep before me; who pay their court in the worn and crumbling pomp of the palace* which stretches its monotonous length on the height; who worship wearily in the stifling air of the churches, urged by no fear or hope, but compelled by their doom to be ever old and undying, to live on in the rigidity of habit, as they live on in perpetual mid-day, without the repose of night or the new birth of morning.

A stunning clang of metal suddenly thrilled through me, and I became conscious of the objects in my room again: one of the fire-irons had fallen as Pierre opened the door to bring me my draught. My heart was palpitating violently, and I begged Pierre to leave my draught beside me; I would take it presently.

As soon as I was alone again, I began to ask myself whether I had been sleeping. Was this a dream—this wonderfully distinct vision—minute in its distinctness down to a patch of rainbow light on the pavement, transmitted through a coloured lamp in the shape of a star—of a strange city, quite unfamiliar to my imagination? I had seen no picture of Prague: it lay in my mind as a mere name, with vaguely-remembered historical associations—ill-defined memories of imperial grandeur and religious wars.

Nothing of this sort had ever occurred in my dreaming experience before, for I had often been humiliated because my dreams were only saved from being utterly disjointed and commonplace by the frequent terrors of nightmare. But I could not believe that I had been asleep, for I remembered distinctly the gradual breaking-in of the vision upon me, like the new images in a dissolving view*, or the growing distinctness of the landscape as the sun lifts up the veil of the morning mist. And while I was conscious of this incipient vision, I was also conscious that Pierre came to tell my father Mr Filmore was waiting for him, and that my father hurried out of the room. No, it was not a dream; was it—the thought was full of tremulous exultation—was it the poet's nature in me, hitherto only a troubled yearning sensibility, now manifesting itself suddenly as spontaneous creation? Surely it was in this way that Homer saw the plain of Troy, that Dante saw the abodes of the departed, that Milton* saw the earthward flight of the Tempter. Was it that my illness had wrought some happy change in my organisation—given a firmer tension to my nerves—carried off some dull obstruction? I had often read of such effects—in works of fiction at least. Nay; in genuine biographies I had read of the subtilising or exalting influence of some diseases on the mental powers. Did not Novalis* feel his inspiration intensified under the progress of consumption?

When my mind had dwelt for some time on this blissful idea, it seemed to me that I might perhaps test it by an exertion of my will. The vision had begun when my father was speaking of our going to Prague. I did not for a moment believe it was really a representation of that city; I believed—I hoped it was a picture that my newly-liberated genius had painted in fiery haste, with the colours snatched from lazy memory. Suppose I were to fix my mind on some other place—Venice, for example, which was far more familiar to my imagination than Prague: perhaps the same sort of result would follow. I concentrated my thoughts on Venice; I stimulated my imagination with poetic memories, and strove to feel myself present in Venice, as I had felt myself present in Prague. But in vain. I was only colouring the Canaletto* engravings that hung in my old bedroom at home; the picture was a shifting one, my mind wandering uncertainly in search of more vivid images; I could see no accident of form or shadow without conscious labour after the necessary conditions. It was all prosaic effort, not rapt passivity, such as

I had experienced half an hour before. I was discouraged; but I remembered that inspiration was fitful.

For several days I was in a state of excited expectation, watching for a recurrence of my new gift. I sent my thoughts ranging over my world of knowledge, in the hope that they would find some object which would send a reawakening vibration through my slumbering genius. But no; my world remained as dim as ever, and that flash of strange light refused to come again, though I watched for it with palpitating eagerness.

My father accompanied me every day in a drive, and a gradually lengthening walk as my powers of walking increased; and one evening he had agreed to come and fetch me at twelve the next day, that we might go together to select a musical box,* and other purchases rigorously demanded of a rich Englishman visiting Geneva. He was one of the most punctual of men and bankers, and I was always nervously anxious to be quite ready for him at the appointed time. But, to my surprise, at a quarter past twelve he had not appeared. I felt all the impatience of a convalescent who has nothing particular to do, and who has just taken a tonic in the prospect of immediate exercise that would carry off the stimulus.

Unable to sit still and reserve my strength, I walked up and down the room, looking out on the current of the Rhone, just where it leaves the dark-blue lake; but thinking all the while of the possible causes that could detain my father.

Suddenly I was conscious that my father was in the room, but not alone: there were two persons with him. Strange! I had heard no footstep, I had not seen the door open; but I saw my father, and at his right hand our neighbour Mrs Filmore, whom I remembered very well, though I had not seen her for five years. She was a commonplace middle-aged woman, in silk and cashmere; but the lady on the left of my father was not more than twenty, a tall, slim, willowy figure, with luxuriant blond hair, arranged in cunning braids and folds that looked almost too massive for the slight figure and the small-featured, thin-lipped face they crowned. But the face had not a girlish expression: the features were sharp, the pale grey eyes at once acute, restless, and sarcastic. They were fixed on me in half-smiling curiosity, and I felt a painful sensation as if a sharp wind were cutting me. The pale-green dress, and the green leaves that seemed to form a border about her pale blond hair, made me think of a Water-Nixie,*

—for my mind was full of German lyrics,* and this pale, fatal-eyed woman, with the green weeds, looked like a birth from some cold, sedgy stream, the daughter of an aged river.]

'Well, Latimer, you thought me long,' my father said. . . .

But while the last word was in my ears, the whole group vanished, and there was nothing between me and the Chinese painted folding-screen that stood before the door. I was cold and trembling; I could only totter forward and throw myself on the sofa. This strange new power had manifested itself again. . . . But *was* it a power? Might it not rather be a disease—a sort of intermittent delirium, concentrating my energy of brain into moments of unhealthy activity, and leaving my saner hours all the more barren? I felt a dizzy sense of unreality in what my eye rested on; I grasped the bell convulsively, like one trying to free himself from nightmare, and rang it twice. Pierre came with a look of alarm in his face.

'Monsieur ne se trouve pas bien?'* he said, anxiously.

'I'm tired of waiting, Pierre,' I said, as distinctly and emphatically as I could, like a man determined to be sober in spite of wine; 'I'm afraid something has happened to my father—he's usually so punctual. Run to the Hôtel des Bergues* and see if he is there.'

Pierre left the room at once, with a soothing 'Bien, Monsieur'; and I felt the better for this scene of simple, waking prose. Seeking to calm myself still further, I went into my bedroom, adjoining the *salon*, and opened a case of eau-de-Cologne; took out a bottle; went through the process of taking out the cork very neatly, and then rubbed the reviving spirit over my hands and forehead, and under my nostrils, drawing a new delight from the scent because I had procured it by slow details of labour, and by no strange sudden madness. Already I had begun to taste something of the horror that belongs to the lot of a human being whose nature is not adjusted to simple human conditions.

Still enjoying the scent, I returned to the *salon*, but it was not unoccupied, as it been before I left it. In front of the Chinese folding-screen there was my father, with Mrs Filmore on his right hand, and on his left——the slim blond-haired girl, with the keen face and the keen eyes fixed on me in half-smiling curiosity.

'Well, Latimer, you thought me long,' my father said. . . .

I heard no more, felt no more, till I became conscious that I was lying with my head low on the sofa, Pierre and my father by my side.

As soon as I was thoroughly revived, my father left the room, and presently returned, saying,

'I've been to tell the ladies how you are, Latimer. They were waiting in the next room. We shall put off our shopping expedition to-day.'

Presently he said, 'That young lady is Bertha Grant, Mrs Filmore's orphan niece. Filmore has adopted her, and she lives with them, so you will have her for a neighbour when we go home—perhaps for a near relation; for there is a tenderness between her and Alfred, I suspect, and I should be gratified by the match, since Filmore means to provide for her in every way as if she were his daughter. It had not occurred to me that you knew nothing about her living with the Filmores.'

He made no further allusion to the fact of my having fainted at the moment of seeing her, and I would not for the world have told him the reason: I shrank from the idea of disclosing to any one what might be regarded as a pitiable peculiarity, most of all from betraying it to my father, who would have suspected my sanity ever after.

I do not mean to dwell with particularity on the details of my experience. I have described these two cases at length, because they had definite, clearly traceable results in my after-lot.

Shortly after this last occurrence—I think the very next day—I began to be aware of a phase in my abnormal sensibility, to which, from the languid and slight nature of my intercourse with others since my illness, I had not been alive before. This was the obtrusion on my mind of the mental process going forward in first one person, and then another, with whom I happened to be in contact: the vagrant, frivolous ideas and emotions of some uninteresting acquaintance—Mrs Filmore, for example—would force themselves on my consciousness like an importunate, ill-played musical instrument, or the loud activity of an imprisoned insect. But this unpleasant sensibility was fitful, and left me moments of rest, when the souls of my companions were once more shut out from me, and I felt a relief such as silence brings to wearied nerves. I might have believed this importunate insight to be merely a diseased activity of the imagination, but that my prevision of incalculable words and actions proved it to have a fixed relation to the mental process in other minds. But this superadded consciousness, wearying and annoying enough when it urged on me the trivial experience of indifferent people, became an intense pain and grief when it seemed to be opening to me the souls of those who were in a close relation to me—when the rational talk, the graceful attentions, the wittily-turned phrases, and the kindly deeds, which used to make the web of their characters, were seen as if thrust asunder by a microscopic vision, that showed all the inter-mediate frivolities, all the suppressed egoism, all the struggling chaos of puerilities, meanness, vague capricious memories, and indo-lent make-shift thoughts, from which human words and deeds emerge like leaflets covering a fermenting heap.

At Basle we were joined by my brother Alfred, now a handsome self-confident man of six-and-twenty—a thorough contrast to my fragile, nervous, ineffectual self. I believe I was held to have a sort of half-womanish, half-ghostly beauty; for the portrait-painters, who are thick as weeds at Geneva,* had often asked me to sit to them, and I had been the model of a dying minstrel in a fancy picture. But I thoroughly disliked my own *physique*, and nothing but the belief that it was a condition of poetic genius would have reconciled me to it. That brief hope was quite fled, and I saw in my face now nothing but the stamp of a morbid organisation, framed for passive suffering—too feeble for the sublime resistance of poetic production. Alfred, from whom I had been almost constantly separated, and who, in his present stage of character and appearance, came before me as a per-fect stranger, was bent on being extremely friendly and brother-like to me. He had the superficial kindness of a good-humoured, self-satisfied nature, that fears no rivalry, and has encountered no contrarieties. I am not sure that my disposition was good enough for me to have been quite free from envy towards him, even if our desires had not clashed, and if I had been in the healthy human condition which admits of generous confidence and charitable con-struction. There must always have been an antipathy between our natures. As it was, he became in a few weeks an object of intense hatred to me; and when he entered the room, still more when he spoke, it was as if a sensation of grating metal had set my teeth on edge. My diseased consciousness was more intensely and continually occupied with his thoughts and emotions, than with those of any other person who came in my way. I was perpetually exasperated with the petty promptings of his conceit and his love of patron-age, with his self-complacent belief in Bertha Grant's passion for him, with his half-pitying contempt for me—seen not in the ordinary indications of intonation and phrase and slight action, which an acute and suspicious mind is on the watch for, but in all their naked skinless complication.

For we were rivals, and our desires clashed, though he was not aware of it. I have said nothing yet of the effect Bertha Grant produced in me on a nearer acquaintance. That effect was chiefly determined by the fact that she made the only exception, among all the human beings about me, to my unhappy gift of insight. About Bertha I was always in a state of uncertainty: I could watch the expression of her face, and speculate on its meaning; I could ask for her opinion with the real interest of ignorance; I could listen for her words and watch for her smile with hope and fear: she had for me the fascination of an unravelled destiny. I say it was this fact that chiefly determined the strong effect she produced on me: for, in the abstract, no womanly character could seem to have less affinity for* that of a shrinking, romantic, passionate youth than Bertha's. She was keen, sarcastic, unimaginative, prematurely cynical, remaining critical and unmoved in the most impressive scenes, inclined to dissect all my favourite poems, and especially contemptuous towards the German lyrics, which were my pet literature at that time. To this moment I am unable to define my feeling towards her: it was not ordinary boyish admiration, for she was the very opposite, even to the colour of her hair, of the ideal woman who still remained to me the type of loveliness; and she was without that enthusiasm for the great and good, which, even at the moment of her strongest dominion over me, I should have declared to be the highest element of character. But there is no tyranny more complete than that which a self-centred negative nature exercises over a morbidly sensitive nature perpetually craving sympathy and support. The most independent people feel the effect of a man's silence in heightening their value for his opinion—feel an additional triumph in conquering the reverence of a critic habitually captious and satirical: no wonder, then, that an enthusiastic self-distrusting youth should watch and wait before the closed secret of a sarcastic woman's face, as if it were the shrine of the doubtfully benignant deity who ruled his destiny. For a young enthusiast is unable to imagine the total negation in another mind of the emotions which are stirring his own: they may be feeble, latent, inactive, he thinks, but they are there—they may be called forth; sometimes, in moments of happy hallucination, he believes they may be there in all the greater strength because he sees no outward sign of them. And this effect, as I have intimated, was heightened to its utmost intensity in me, because Bertha was the only being who remained for me in the mysterious seclusion of soul that renders such youthful delusion possible. Doubtless there was another sort of fascination at work—that subtle physical attraction which delights in cheating our psychological predictions, and in compelling the men who paint sylphs, to fall in love with some *bonne et brave femme*,* heavy-heeled and freckled.

Bertha's behaviour towards me was such as to encourage all my illusions, to heighten my boyish passion, and make me more and more dependent on her smiles. Looking back with my present wretched knowledge, I conclude that her vanity and love of power were intensely gratified by the belief that I had fainted on first seeing her purely from the strong impression her person had produced on me. The most prosaic woman likes to believe herself the object of a violent, a poetic passion; and without a grain of romance in her, Bertha had that spirit of intrigue which gave piquancy to the idea that the brother of the man she meant to marry was dying with love and jealousy for her sake. That she meant to marry my brother, was what at that time I did not believe; for though he was assiduous in his attentions to her, and I knew well enough that both he and my father had made up their minds to this result, there was not yet an understood engagement—there had been no explicit declaration; and Bertha habitually, while she flirted with my brother, and accepted his homage in a way that implied to him a thorough recognition of its intention, made me believe, by the subtlest looks and phrases—feminine nothings which could never be quoted against her—that he was really the object of her secret ridicule, that she thought him, as I did, a coxcomb, whom she would have pleasure in disappointing. Me she openly petted in my brother's presence, as if I were too young and sickly ever to be thought of as a lover; and that was the view he took of me. But I believe she must inwardly have delighted in the tremors into which she threw me by the coaxing way in which she patted my curls, while she laughed at my quotations. Such caresses were always given in the presence of our friends; for when we were alone together, she affected a much greater distance towards me, and now and then took the opportunity, by words or slight actions, to stimulate my foolish timid hope that she really preferred me. And why should she not follow her inclination? I was not in so advantageous a position as my brother, but I had fortune, I was not a year younger than she was, and she was an heiress, who would soon be of age to decide for herself.

The fluctuations of hope and fear, confined to this one channel, made each day in her presence a delicious torment. There was one deliberate act of hers which especially helped to intoxicate me. When we were at Vienna her twentieth birthday occurred, and as she was very fond of ornaments, we all took the opportunity of the splendid jewellers' shops in that Teutonic Paris to purchase her a birthday present of jewellery. Mine, naturally, was the least expensive; it was an opal* ring—the opal was my favourite stone, because it seems to blush and turn pale as if it had a soul. I told Bertha so when I gave it her, and said that it was an emblem of the poetic nature, changing with the changing light of heaven and of woman's eyes. In the evening she appeared elegantly dressed, and wearing conspicuously all the birthday presents except mine. I looked eagerly at her fingers, but saw no opal. I had no opportunity of noticing this to her during the evening; but the next day, when I found her seated near the window alone, after breakfast, I said, 'You scorn to wear my poor opal. I should have remembered that you despised poetic natures, and should have given you coral, or turquoise, or some other opaque unresponsive stone.' 'Do I despise it?' she answered, taking hold of a delicate gold chain which she always wore round her neck and drawing out the end from her bosom with my ring hanging to it; 'it hurts me a little, I can tell you,' she said, with her usual dubious smile, 'to wear it in that secret place; and since your poetical nature is so stupid as to prefer a more public position, I shall not endure the pain any longer.'

She took off the ring from the chain and put it on her finger, smiling still, while the blood rushed to my cheeks, and I could not trust myself to say a word of entreaty that she would keep the ring where it was before.

I was completely fooled by this, and for two days shut myself up in my own room whenever Bertha was absent, that I might intoxicate myself afresh with the thought of this scene, and all it implied.

I should mention that during these two months—which seemed a long life to me from the novelty and intensity of the pleasures and pains I underwent—my diseased participation in other people's consciousness continued to torment me; now it was my father, and now my brother, now Mrs Filmore or her husband, and now our German courier, whose stream of thought rushed upon me like a ringing in the ears not to be got rid of, though it allowed my own impulses and ideas to continue their uninterrupted course. It was like a preternaturally heightened sense of hearing, making audible to one a roar of sound where others find perfect stillness. The weariness and disgust of this involuntary intrusion into other souls was counteracted only by my ignorance of Bertha, and my growing passion for her; a passion enormously stimulated, if not produced, by that ignorance. She was my oasis of mystery in the dreary desert of knowledge. I had never allowed my diseased condition to betray itself, or to drive me into any unusual speech or action, except once, when, in a moment of peculiar bitterness against my brother, I had forestalled some words which I knew he was going to utter—a clever observation, which he had prepared beforehand. He had occasionally a slightly-affected hesitation in his speech, and when he paused an instant after the second word, my impatience and jealousy impelled me to continue the speech for him, as if it were something we had both learned by rote. He coloured and looked astonished, as well as annoyed; and the words had no sooner escaped my lips than I felt a shock of alarm lest such an anticipation of words—very far from being words of course, easy to divine—should have betrayed me as an exceptional being, a sort of quiet energumen,* whom every one, Bertha above all, would shudder at and avoid. But I magnified, as usual, the impression any word or deed of mine could produce on others; for no one gave any sign of having noticed my interruption as more than a rudeness, to be forgiven me on the score of my feeble nervous condition.

While this superadded consciousness of the actual was almost constant with me, I had never had a recurrence of that distinct prevision which I have described in relation to my first interview with Bertha; and I was waiting with eager curiosity to know whether or not my vision of Prague would prove to have been an instance of the same kind. A few days after the incident of the opal ring, we were paying one of our frequent visits to the Lichtenberg Palace.* I could never look at many pictures in succession; for pictures, when they are at all powerful, affect me so strongly that one or two exhaust all my capability of contemplation. This morning I had been looking at Giorgione's picture* of the cruel-eyed woman, said to be a likeness of

Lucrezia Borgia, I had stood long alone before it, fascinated by the terrible reality of that cunning, relentless face, till I felt a strange poisoned sensation, as if I had long been inhaling a fatal odour, and was just beginning to be conscious of its effects. Perhaps even then I should not have moved away, if the rest of the party had not returned to this room, and announced that they were going to the Belvedere Gallery* to settle a bet which had arisen between my brother and Mr Filmore about a portrait. I followed them dreamily, and was hardly alive to what occurred till they had all gone up to the gallery, leaving me below; for I refused to come within sight of another picture that day. I made my way to the Grand Terrace,* for it was agreed that we should saunter in the gardens when the dispute had been decided. I had been sitting here a short space, vaguely conscious of trim gardens, with a city and green hills in the distance, when, wishing to avoid the proximity of the sentinel, I rose and walked down the broad stone steps, intending to seat myself farther on in the gardens. Just as I reached the gravel-walk, I felt an arm slipped within mine, and a light hand gently pressing my wrist. In the same instant a strange intoxicating numbness passed over me, like the continuance or climax of the sensation I was still feeling from the gaze of Lucrezia Borgia. The gardens, the summer sky, the consciousness of Bertha's arm being within mine, all vanished, and I seemed to be suddenly in darkness, out of which there gradually broke a dim firelight, and I felt myself sitting in my father's leather chair in the library at home. I knew the fireplace—the dogs* for the wood-fire—the black marble chimney-piece with the white marble medallion of the dying Cleopatra in the centre. Intense and hopeless misery was pressing on my soul; the light became stronger, for Bertha was entering with a candle in her hand—Bertha, my wife—with cruel eyes, with green jewels and green leaves on her white ball-dress; every hateful thought within her present to me ... 'Madman, idiot! why don't you kill yourself, then?' It was a moment of hell. I saw into her pitiless soul—saw its barren worldliness, its scorching hate—and felt it clothe me round like an air I was obliged to breathe. She came with her candle and stood over me with a bitter smile of contempt; I saw the great emerald brooch on her bosom, a studded serpent with diamond eyes. I shuddered—I despised this woman with the barren soul and mean thoughts; but I felt helpless before her, as if she clutched my bleeding heart, and would clutch it till the last drop of life-blood ebbed away. She was my wife, and we hated each other. Gradually the hearth, the dim library, the candle-light disappeared—seemed to melt away into a background of light, the green serpent with the diamond eyes remaining a dark image on the retina. Then I had a sense of my eyelids quivering, and the living daylight broke in upon me; I saw gardens, and heard voices; I was seated on the steps of the Belvedere Terrace, and my friends were round me.

The tumult of mind into which I was thrown by this hideous vision made me ill for several days, and prolonged our stay at Vienna. I shuddered with horror as the scene recurred to me; and it recurred constantly, with all its minutiæ, as if they had been burnt into my memory; and yet, such is the madness of the human heart under the influence of its immediate desires, I felt a wild hell-braving joy that Bertha was to be mine; for the fulfilment of my former prevision concerning her first appearance before me, left me little hope that this last hideous glimpse of the future was the mere diseased play of my own mind, and had no relation to external realities. One thing alone I looked towards as a possible means of casting doubt on my terrible conviction—the discovery that my vision of Prague had been false—and Prague was the next city on our route.

Meanwhile, I was no sooner in Bertha's society again, than I was as completely under her sway as before. What if I saw into the heart of Bertha, the matured woman—Bertha, my wife? Bertha, the *girl*, was a fascinating secret to me still: I trembled under her touch; I felt the witchery of her presence; I yearned to be assured of her love. The fear of poison is feeble against the sense of thirst. Nay, I was just as jealous of my brother as before— just as much irritated by his small patronising ways; for my pride, my diseased sensibility, were there as they had always been, and winced as inevitably under every offence as my eye winced from an intruding mote. The future, even when brought within the compass of feeling by a vision that made me shudder, had still no more than the force of an idea, compared with the force of present emotion—of my love for Bertha, of my dislike and jealousy towards my brother.

It is an old story,* that men sell themselves to the tempter, and sign a bond with their blood, because it is only to take effect at a distant day; then rush on to snatch the cup their souls thirst after with an impulse not less savage because there is a dark shadow beside them for evermore. There is no short cut, no patent tram-road,* to wisdom: after all the centuries of invention, the soul's path lies through the thorny wilderness* which must be still trodden in solitude, with bleeding feet, with sobs for help, as it was trodden by them of old time.

My mind speculated eagerly on the means by which I should become my brother's successful rival, for I was still too timid, in my ignorance of Bertha's actual feeling, to venture on any step that would urge from her an avowal of it. I thought I should gain confidence even for this, if my vision of Prague proved to have been veracious; and yet, the horror of that certitude! Behind the slim girl Bertha, whose words and looks I watched for, whose touch was bliss, there stood continually that Bertha with the fuller form, the harder eyes, the more rigid mouth,—with the barren selfish soul laid bare; no longer a fascinating secret, but a measured fact, urging itself perpetually on my unwilling sight. Are you unable to give me your sympathy—you who read this? Are you unable to imagine this double consciousness* at work within me, flowing on like two parallel streams that never mingle their waters and blend into a common hue? Yet you must have known something of the presentiments that spring from an insight at war with passion; and my visions were only like presentiments intensified to horror. You have known the powerlessness of ideas before the might of impulse; and my visions, when once they had passed into memory, were mere ideas—pale shadows, that beckoned in vain, while my hand was grasped by the living and the loved.

In after-days I thought with bitter regret that if I had foreseen something more or something different—if instead of that hideous vision which poisoned the passion it could not destroy, or if even along with it I could have had a foreshadowing of that moment when I looked on my brother's face for the last time, some softening influence would have been shed over my feeling towards him: pride and hatred would surely have been subdued into pity, and the record of those hidden sins would have been shortened. But this is one of the vain thoughts with which we men flatter ourselves. We try to believe that the egoism within us would have easily been melted, and that it was only the narrowness of our knowledge which hemmed in our generosity, our awe, our human piety, and hindered them from submerging our hard indifference to the sensations and emotions of our fellow. Our tenderness and self-renunciation seem strong when our egoism has had its day*—when, after our mean striving for a triumph that is to be another's loss, the triumph comes suddenly, and we shudder at it, because it is held out by the chill hand of death.

Our arrival in Prague happened at night, and I was glad of this, for it seemed like a deferring of a terribly decisive moment, to be in the city for hours without seeing it. As we were not to remain long in Prague, but to go on speedily to Dresden, it was proposed that we should drive out the next morning and take a general view of the place, as well as visit some of its specially interesting spots, before the heat became oppressive—for we were in August, and the season was hot and dry. But it happened that the ladies were rather late at their morning toilet, and to my father's politely-repressed but perceptible annoyance, we were not in the carriage till the morning was far advanced. I thought with a sense of relief, as we entered the Jews' quarter, where we were to visit the old synagogue,* that we should be kept in this flat, shut-up part of the city, until we should all be too tired and too warm to go farther, and so we should return without seeing more than the streets through which we had already passed. That would give me another day's suspense—suspense, the only form in which a fearful spirit knows the solace of hope. But, as I stood under the blackened, groined arches of that old synagogue, made dimly visible by the seven thin candles in the sacred lamp, while our Jewish cicerone* reached down the Book of the Law, and read to us in its ancient tongue,—I felt a shuddering impression that this strange building, with its shrunken lights, this surviving withered remnant of medieval Judaism, was of a piece with my vision. Those darkened dusty Christian saints, with their loftier arches and their larger candles, needed the consolatory scorn with which they might point to a more shrivelled death-in-life than their own.

As I expected, when we left the Jews' quarter, the elders of our party wished to return to the hotel. But now, instead of rejoicing in this, as I had done beforehand, I felt a sudden overpowering impulse to go on at once to the bridge, and put an end to the suspense I had been wishing to protract. I declared, with unusual decision, that I would get out of the carriage and walk on alone; they might return without me. My father, thinking this merely a sample of my usual 'poetic nonsense', objected that I should only do myself harm by walking in the heat; but when I persisted, he said angrily that I might follow my own absurd devices, but that Schmidt (our courier) must go with me. I assented to this, and set off with Schmidt towards the bridge. I had no sooner passed from under the archway of the grand old gate leading on to the bridge, than a trembling seized me, and I turned cold under the mid-day sun; yet I went on; I was in search of something—a small detail which I remembered with special intensity as part of my vision. There it was—the patch of rainbow light on the pavement transmitted through a lamp in the shape of a star.

CHAPTER II

BEFORE the autumn was at an end, and while the brown leaves still stood thick on the beeches in our park, my brother and Bertha were engaged to each other, and it was understood that their marriage was to take place early in the next spring. In spite of the certainty I had felt from that moment on the bridge at Prague, that Bertha would one day be my wife, my constitutional timidity and distrust had continued to benumb me, and the words in which I had sometimes premeditated a confession of my love, had died away unuttered. The same conflict had gone on within me as before—the longing for an assurance of love from Bertha's lips, the dread lest a word of contempt and denial should fall upon me like a corrosive acid. What was the conviction of a distant necessity to me? I trembled under a present glance, I hungered after a present joy, I was clogged and chilled by a present fear. And so the days passed on: I witnessed Bertha's engagement and heard her marriage discussed as if I were under a conscious nightmare—knowing it was a dream that would vanish, but feeling stifled under the grasp of hard-clutching fingers.

When I was not in Bertha's presence—and I was with her very often, for she continued to treat me with a playful patronage that wakened no jealousy in my brother—I spent my time chiefly in wandering, in strolling, or taking long rides while the daylight lasted, and then shutting myself up with my unread books; for books had lost the power of chaining my attention. My self-consciousness was heightened to that pitch of intensity in which our own emotions take the form of a drama which urges itself imperatively on our contemplation, and we begin to weep, less under the sense of our suffering than at the thought of it. I felt a sort of pitying anguish over the pathos of my own lot: the lot of a being finely organised for pain, but with hardly any fibres that responded to pleasure—to whom the idea of future evil robbed the present of its joy, and for whom the idea of future good did not still the uneasiness of a present yearning or a present dread. I went dumbly through that stage of the poet's suffering, in which he feels the delicious pang of utterance, and makes an image of his sorrows.

I was left entirely without remonstrance concerning this dreamy

Poet's suffering

wayward life: I knew my father's thought about me: 'That lad will never be good for anything in life: he may waste his years in an insignificant way on the income that falls to him: I shall not trouble myself about a career for him.'

One mild morning in the beginning of November, it happened that I was standing outside the portico patting lazy old Cæsar, a Newfoundland almost blind with age, the only dog that ever took any notice of me—for the very dogs shunned me, and fawned on the happier people about me—when the groom brought up my brother's horse which was to carry him to the hunt, and my brother himself appeared at the door, florid, broad-chested, and self-complacent, feeling what a good-natured fellow he was not to behave insolently to us all on the strength of his great advantages.

'Latimer, old boy,' he said to me in a tone of compassionate cordiality, 'what a pity it is you don't have a run with the hounds now and then! The finest thing in the world for low spirits!'

'Low spirits!' I thought bitterly, as he rode away; 'that is the sort of phrase with which coarse, narrow natures like yours think to describe experience of which you can know no more than your horse knows. It is to such as you that the good of this world falls: ready dulness, healthy selfishness, good-tempered conceit—these are the keys to happiness.'

The quick thought came, that my selfishness was even stronger than his—it was only a suffering selfishness instead of an enjoying one. But then, again, my exasperating insight into Alfred's self-complacent soul, his freedom from all the doubts and fears, the unsatisfied yearnings, the exquisite tortures of sensitiveness, that had made the web of my life, seemed to absolve me from all bonds towards him. This man needed no pity, no love; those fine influences would have been as little felt by him as the delicate white mist is felt by the rock it caresses. There was no evil in store for *him*: if he was not to marry Bertha, it would be because he had found a lot pleasanter to himself.

Mr Filmore's house lay not more than half a mile beyond our own gates, and whenever I knew my brother was gone in another direction, I went there for the chance of finding Bertha at home. Later on in the day I walked thither. By a rare accident she was alone, and we walked out in the grounds together, for she seldom went on foot beyond the trimly-swept gravel-walks. I remember what a beautiful sylph she looked to me as the low November sun shone on her blond hair, and she tripped along teasing me with her usual light banter, to which I listened half fondly, half moodily; it was all the sign Bertha's mysterious inner self ever made to me. To-day perhaps the moodiness predominated, for I had not yet shaken off the access of jealous hate which my brother had raised in me by his parting patronage. Suddenly I interrupted and startled her by saying, almost fiercely, 'Bertha, how can you love Alfred?'

She looked at me with surprise for a moment, but soon her light smile came again, and she answered sarcastically, 'Why do you suppose I love him?'

'How can you ask that, Bertha?'

'What! your wisdom thinks I must love the man I'm going to marry? The most unpleasant thing in the world. I should quarrel with him; I should be jealous of him; our *ménage* would be conducted in a very ill-bred manner. A little quiet contempt contributes greatly to the elegance of life.'

'Bertha, that is not your real feeling. Why do you delight in trying to deceive me by inventing such cynical speeches?'

'I need never take the trouble of invention in order to deceive you, my small Tasso'*—(that was the mocking name she usually gave me). 'The easiest way to deceive a poet is to tell him the truth.'

She was testing the validity of her epigram in a daring way, and for a moment the shadow of my vision—the Bertha whose soul was no secret to me—passed between me and the radiant girl, the playful sylph whose feelings were a fascinating mystery. I suppose I must have shuddered, or betrayed in some other way my momentary chill of horror.

'Tasso!' she said, seizing my wrist, and peeping round into my face, 'are you really beginning to discern what a heartless girl I am? Why, you are not half the poet I thought you were; you are actually capable of believing the truth about me.'

The shadow passed from between us, and was no longer the object nearest to me. The girl whose light fingers grasped me, whose elfish charming face looked into mine—who, I thought, was betraying an interest in my feelings that she would not have directly avowed,—this warm-breathing presence again possessed my senses and imagination like a returning syren melody which had been overpowered for an instant by the roar of threatening waves. It was a moment as delicious to me as the waking up to a consciousness of youth after a dream of middle age. I forgot everything but my passion, and said with swimming eyes—

'Bertha, shall you love me when we are first married? I wouldn't mind if you really loved me only for a little while.'

Her look of astonishment, as she loosed my hand and started away from me recalled me to a sense of my strange, my criminal indiscretion.

'Forgive me,' I said, hurriedly, as soon as I could speak again; 'I did not know what I was saying.'

'Ah, Tasso's mad fit has come on, I see,' she answered quietly, for she had recovered herself sooner than I had. 'Let him go home and keep his head cool. I must go in, for the sun is setting.'

I left her—full of indignation against myself. I had let slip words which, if she reflected on them, might rouse in her a suspicion of my abnormal mental condition—a suspicion which of all things I dreaded. And besides that, I was ashamed of the apparent baseness I had committed in uttering them to my brother's betrothed wife. I wandered home slowly, entering our park through a private gate instead of by the lodges. As I approached the house, I saw a man dashing off at full speed from the stable-yard across the park. Had any accident happened at home? No; perhaps it was only one of my father's peremptory business errands that required this headlong haste. Nevertheless I quickened my pace without any distinct motive, and was soon at the house. I will not dwell on the scene I found there. My brother was dead—had been pitched from his horse, and killed on the spot by a concussion of the brain.

I went up to the room where he lay, and where my father was seated beside him with a look of rigid despair. I had shunned my father more than any one since our return home, for the radical antipathy between our natures made my insight into his inner self a constant affliction to me. But now, as I went up to him, and stood beside him in sad silence, I felt the presence of a new element that blended us as we had never been blent before. My father had been one of the most successful men in the money-getting world: he had had no sentimental sufferings, no illness. The heaviest trouble that had befallen him was the death of his first wife. But he married my mother soon after; and I remember he seemed exactly the same, to my keen childish observation, the week after her death as before. But now, at last, a sorrow had come—the sorrow of old age, which suffers the more from the crushing of its pride and its hopes, in proportion as the pride and hope are narrow and prosaic. His son was to have been married soon—would probably have stood for the borough at the next election. That son's existence was the best motive that could be alleged for making new purchases of land every year to round off the estate. It is a dreary thing to live on doing the same things year after year, without knowing why we do them. <u>Perhaps the tragedy of disappointed youth and passion is less piteous than the tragedy of disappointed age and worldliness</u>.

As I saw into the desolation of my father's heart, I felt a movement of deep pity towards him, which was the beginning of a new affection—an affection that grew and strengthened in spite of the strange bitterness with which he regarded me in the first month or two after my brother's death. If it had not been for the softening influence of my compassion for him—the first deep compassion I had ever felt—I should have been stung by the perception that my father transferred the inheritance of an eldest son to me with a mortified sense that fate had compelled him to the unwelcome course of caring for me as an important being. It was only in spite of himself that he began to think of me with anxious regard. There is hardly any neglected child for whom death has made vacant a more favoured place, who will not understand what I mean.

Gradually, however, my new deference to his wishes, the effect of that patience which was born of my pity for him, won upon his affection, and he began to please himself with the endeavour to make me fill my brother's place as fully as my feebler personality would admit. I saw that the prospect which by-and-by presented itself of my becoming Bertha's husband was welcome to him, and he even contemplated in my case what he had not intended in my brother's—that his son and daughter-in-law should make one household with him. My softened feeling towards my father made this the happiest time I had known since childhood;—these last months in which I retained the delicious illusion of loving Bertha, of longing and doubting and hoping that she might love me. She behaved with a certain new consciousness and distance towards me after my brother's death; and I too was under a double constraint—that of delicacy towards my brother's memory, and of anxiety as to the impression my abrupt words had left on her mind. But the additional screen this mutual reserve erected between us only brought me more completely under her power: no matter how empty the adytum,* so that the veil be thick enough. So absolute is our soul's need of something hidden and uncertain for the maintenance of that doubt and hope and effort which are the breath of its life, that if the whole future were laid bare to us beyond to-day, the interest of all mankind would be bent on the hours that lie between; we should pant after the uncertainties of our one morning and our one afternoon; we should rush fiercely to the Exchange for our last possibility of speculation, of success, of disappointment; we should have a glut of political prophets foretelling a crisis or a no-crisis within the only twenty-four hours left open to prophecy. Conceive the condition of the human mind if all propositions whatsoever were self-evident except one, which was to become self-evident at the close of a summer's day, but in the meantime might be the subject of question, of hypothesis, of debate. Art and philosophy, literature and science, would fasten like bees on that one proposition which had the honey of probability in it, and be the more eager because their enjoyment would end with sunset. Our impulses, our spiritual activities, no more adjust themselves to the idea of their future nullity, than the beating of our heart, or the irritability of our muscles.

Bertha, the slim, fair-haired girl, whose present thoughts and emotions were an enigma to me amidst the fatiguing obviousness of the other minds around me, was as absorbing to me as a single unknown to-day—as a single hypothetic proposition to remain problematic till sunset; and all the cramped, hemmed-in belief and disbelief, trust and distrust, of my nature, welled out in this one narrow channel.

And she made me believe that she loved me. Without ever quitting her tone of *badinage* and playful superiority, she intoxicated me with the sense that I was necessary to her, that she was never at ease unless I was near her, submitting to her playful tyranny. It costs a woman so little effort to besot us in this way! A half-repressed word, a moment's unexpected silence, even an easy fit of petulance on our account, will serve us as *hashish** for a long while. Out of the subtlest web of scarcely perceptible signs, she set me weaving the fancy that she had always unconsciously loved me better than Alfred, but that, with the ignorant fluttered sensibility of a young girl, she had been imposed on by the charm that lay for her in the distinction of being admired and chosen by a man who made so brilliant a figure in the world as my brother. She satirised herself in a very graceful way for her vanity and ambition. What was it to me that I had the light of my wretched prevision on the fact that now it was I who possessed at least all but the personal part of my brother's advantages? Our sweet illusions are half of them conscious illusions, like effects of colour that we know to be made up of tinsel, broken glass, and rags.

We were married eighteen months after Alfred's death, one cold, clear morning in April, when there came hail and sunshine both together; and Bertha, in her white silk and pale-green leaves, and the pale hues of her hair and face, looked like the spirit of the morning. My father was happier than he had thought of being again: my marriage, he felt sure, would complete the desirable modification of my character, and make me practical and worldly enough to take my place in society among sane men. For he delighted in Bertha's tact and acuteness, and felt sure she would be mistress of me, and make me what she chose: I was only twenty-one, and madly in love with her. Poor father! He kept that hope a little while after our first year of marriage, and it was not quite extinct when paralysis came and saved him from utter disappointment.

I shall hurry through the rest of my story, not dwelling so much as I have hitherto done on my inward experience. When people are well known to each other, they talk rather of what befals them externally, leaving their feelings and sentiments to be inferred.

We lived in a round of visits for some time after our return home, giving splendid dinner-parties, and making a sensation in our neighbourhood by the new lustre of our equipage, for my father had reserved this display of his increased wealth for the period of his son's marriage; and we gave our acquaintances liberal opportunity for remarking that it was a pity I made so poor a figure as an heir and a bridegroom. The nervous fatigue of this existence, the insincerities and platitudes which I had to live through twice over—through my inner and outward sense—would have been maddening to me, if I had not had that sort of intoxicated callousness which came from the delights of a first passion. A bride and bridegroom, surrounded by all the appliances of wealth, hurried through the day by the whirl of society, filling their solitary moments with hastily-snatched caresses, are prepared for their future life together as the novice is prepared for the cloister, by experiencing its utmost contrast.

Through all these crowded excited months, Bertha's inward self remained shrouded from me, and I still read her thoughts only through the language of her lips and demeanour: I had still the human interest of wondering whether what I did and said pleased her, of longing to hear a word of affection, of giving a delicious exaggeration of meaning to her smile. But I was conscious of a growing difference in her manner towards me; sometimes strong enough to be called haughty coldness, cutting and chilling me as the hail had done that came across the sunshine on our marriage morning; sometimes only perceptible in the dexterous avoidance of a *tête-à-tête* walk or dinner to which I had been looking forward. I had been deeply pained by this—had even felt a sort of crushing of the heart, from the sense that my brief day of happiness was near its setting; but still I remained dependent on Bertha, eager for the last rays of a bliss that would soon be gone for ever, hoping and watching for some after-glow more beautiful from the impending night.

I remember—how should I not remember?—the time when that dependence and hope utterly left me, when the sadness I had felt in Bertha's growing estrangement became a joy that I looked back upon with longing, as a man might look back on the last pains in a para-lysed limb. It was just after the close of my father's last illness, which had necessarily withdrawn us from society and thrown us more upon each other. It was the evening of my father's death. On that evening the veil which had shrouded Bertha's soul from me—had made me find in her alone among my fellow-beings the blessed possibility of mystery, and doubt, and expectation—was first withdrawn. Perhaps it was the first day since the beginning of my passion for her, in which that passion was completely neutralised by the presence of an absorbing feeling of another kind. I had been watching by my father's death-bed: I had been witnessing the last fitful yearning glance his soul had cast back on the spent inheritance of life—the last faint consciousness of love he had gathered from the pressure of my hand. What are all our personal loves when we have been sharing in that supreme agony? In the first moments when we come away from the presence of death, every other relation to the living is merged, to our feeling, in the great relation of a common nature and a common destiny.

In that state of mind I joined Bertha in her private sitting-room.

She was seated in a leaning posture on a settee, with her back towards the door; the great rich coils of her pale blond hair surmounting her small neck, visible above the back of the settee. I remember, as I closed the door behind me, a cold tremulousness seizing me, and a vague sense of being hated and lonely—vague and strong, like a presentiment. I know how I looked at that moment, for I saw myself in Bertha's thought as she lifted her cutting grey eyes, and looked at me: a miserable ghost-seer, surrounded by phantoms in the noon-day, trembling under a breeze when the leaves were still, without appetite for the common objects of human desire, but pining after the moonbeams. We were front to front with each other, and judged each other. The terrible moment of complete illumination had come to me, and I saw that the darkness had hidden no landscape from me, but only a blank prosaic wall: from that evening forth, through the sickening years which followed, I saw all round the narrow room of this woman's soul—saw petty artifice and mere negation where I had delighted to believe in coy sensibilities and in wit at war with latent feeling—saw the light floating vanities of the girl defining themselves into the systematic coquetry, the scheming selfishness, of the woman—saw repulsion and antipathy harden into cruel hatred, giving pain only for the sake of wreaking itself.

For Bertha too, after her kind, felt the bitterness of disillusion. She had believed that my wild poet's passion for her would make me her slave; and that, being her slave, I should execute her will in all things. With the essential shallowness of a negative, unimaginative nature, she was unable to conceive the fact that sensibilities were anything else than weaknesses. She had thought my weaknesses would put me in her power, and she found them unmanageable forces. Our positions were reversed. Before marriage she had completely mastered my imagination, for she was a secret to me; and I created the unknown thought before which I trembled as if it were hers. But now that her soul was laid open to me, now that I was compelled to share the privacy of her motives, to follow all the petty devices that preceded her words and acts, she found herself powerless with me, except to produce in me the chill shudder of repulsion—powerless, because I could be acted on by no lever within her reach. I was dead to worldly ambitions, to social vanities, to all the incentives within the compass of her narrow imagination, and I lived under influences utterly invisible to her.

She was really pitiable to have such a husband, and so all the world thought. A graceful, brilliant woman, like Bertha, who smiled on morning callers, made a figure in ball-rooms, and was capable of that light repartee which, from such a woman, is accepted as wit, was secure of carrying off all sympathy from a husband who was sickly, abstracted, and, as some suspected, crack-brained. Even the servants in our house gave her the balance of their regard and pity. For there were no audible quarrels between us; our alienation, our repulsion from each other, lay within the silence of our own hearts; and if the mistress went out a great deal, and seemed to dislike the master's society, was it not natural, poor thing? The master was odd. I was kind and just to my dependants, but I excited in them a shrinking, half-contemptuous pity; for this class of men and women are but slightly determined in their estimate of others by general considerations, or even experience, of character. They judge of persons as they judge of coins, and value those who pass current at a high rate.

After a time I interfered so little with Bertha's habits, that it might seem wonderful how her hatred towards me could grow so intense and active as it did. But she had begun to suspect, by some involuntary betrayals of mine, that there was an abnormal power of penetration in me—that fitfully, at least, I was strangely cognisant of her thoughts and intentions, and she began to be haunted by a terror of me, which alternated every now and then with defiance. She meditated continually how the incubus* could be shaken off her life—how she could be freed from this hateful bond to a being whom she at once despised as an imbecile, and dreaded as an inquisitor. For a long while she lived in the hope that my evident wretchedness would drive me to the commission of suicide; but suicide was not in my nature. I was too completely swayed by the sense that I was in the grasp of unknown forces, to believe in my power of self-release. Towards my own destiny I had become entirely passive; for my one ardent desire had spent itself, and impulse no longer predominated over knowledge. For this reason I never thought of taking any steps towards a complete separation, which would have made our alienation evident to the world. Why should I rush for help to a new course, when I was only suffering from the consequences of a deed which had been the act of my intensest will? That would have been the logic of one who had desires to gratify, and I had no desires. But

Bertha and I lived more and more aloof from each other. The rich find it easy to live married and apart.

That course of our life which I have indicated in a few sentences filled the space of years. So much misery—so slow and hideous a growth of hatred and sin, may be compressed into a sentence! And men judge of each other's lives through this summary medium. They epitomise the experience of their fellow-mortal, and pronounce judgment on him in neat syntax, and feel themselves wise and virtuous—conquerors over the temptations they define in well-selected predicates. Seven years of wretchedness glide glibly over the lips of the man who has never counted them out in moments of chill disappointment, of head and heart throbbings, of dread and vain wrestling, of remorse and despair. We learn *words* by rote, but not their meaning; *that* must be paid for with our life-blood, and printed in the subtle fibres of our nerves.

But I will hasten to finish my story. Brevity is justified at once to those who readily understand, and to those who will never understand.

Some years after my father's death, I was sitting by the dim firelight in my library one January evening—sitting in the leather chair that used to be my father's—when Bertha appeared at the door, with a candle in her hand, and advanced towards me. I knew the ball-dress she had on—the white ball-dress, with the green jewels, shone upon by the light of the wax candle which lit up the medallion of the dying Cleopatra on the mantelpiece. Why did she come to me before going out? I had not seen her in the library, which was my habitual place, for months. Why did she stand before me with the candle in her hand, with her cruel contemptuous eyes fixed on me, and the glittering serpent, like a familiar demon, on her breast? For a moment I thought this fulfilment of my vision at Vienna marked some dreadful crisis in my fate, but I saw nothing in Bertha's mind, as she stood before me, except scorn for the look of overwhelming misery with which I sat before her. . . . 'Fool, idiot, why don't you kill yourself, then?'—that was her thought. But at length her thoughts reverted to her errand, and she spoke aloud. The apparently indifferent nature of the errand seemed to make a ridiculous anticlimax to my prevision and my agitation.

'I have had to hire a new maid. Fletcher is going to be married, and she wants me to ask you to let her husband have the public-house and farm at Molton. I wish him to have it. You must give the promise now, because Fletcher is going to-morrow morning—and quickly, because I'm in a hurry.'

'Very well; you may promise her,' I said, indifferently, and Bertha swept out of the library again.

I always shrank from the sight of a new person, and all the more when it was a person whose mental life was likely to weary my reluctant insight with worldly ignorant trivialities. But I shrank especially from the sight of this new maid, because her advent had been announced to me at a moment to which I could not cease to attach some fatality: I had a vague dread that I should find her mixed up with the dreary drama of my life—that some new sickening vision would reveal her to me as an evil genius. When at last I did unavoidably meet her, the vague dread was changed into definite disgust. She was a tall, wiry, dark-eyed woman, this Mrs Archer, with a face handsome enough to give her coarse hard nature the odious finish of bold, self-confident coquetry. That was enough to make me avoid her, quite apart from the contemptuous feeling with which she contemplated me. I seldom saw her; but I perceived that she rapidly became a favourite with her mistress, and, after the lapse of eight or nine months, I began to be aware that there had arisen in Bertha's mind towards this woman a mingled feeling of fear and dependence, and that this feeling was associated with ill-defined images of candle-light scenes in her dressing-room, and the locking-up of something in Bertha's cabinet. My interviews with my wife had become so brief and so rarely solitary, that I had no opportunity of perceiving these images in her mind with more definiteness. The recollections of the past become contracted in the rapidity of thought till they sometimes bear hardly a more distinct resemblance to the external reality than the forms of an oriental alphabet to the objects that suggested them.

Besides, for the last year or more a modification had been going forward in my mental condition, and was growing more and more marked. My insight into the minds of those around me was becoming dimmer and more fitful, and the ideas that crowded my double consciousness became less and less dependent on any personal contact. All that was personal in me seemed to be suffering a gradual death, so that I was losing the organ through which the personal agitations and projects of others could affect me. But along with this relief from wearisome insight, there was a new development of what I concluded—as I have since found rightly—to be a prevision of external scenes. It was as if the relation between me and my fellow-men was more and more deadened, and my relation to what we call the inanimate was quickened into new life. The more I lived apart from society, and in proportion as my wretchedness subsided from the violent throb of agonised passion into the dullness of habitual pain, the more frequent and vivid became such visions as that I had had of Prague—of strange cities, of sandy plains, of gigantic ruins, of midnight skies with strange bright constellations, of mountain-passes, of grassy nooks flecked with the afternoon sunshine through the boughs: I was in the midst of such scenes, and in all of them one presence seemed to weigh on me in all these mighty shapes—the presence of something unknown and pitiless. For continual suffering had annihilated religious faith within me: to the utterly miserable—the unloving and the unloved—there is no religion possible, no worship, but a worship of devils. And beyond all these, and continually recurring, was the vision of my death—the pangs, the suffocation, the last struggle, when life would be grasped at in vain.

Things were in this state near the end of the seventh year. I had become entirely free from insight, from my abnormal cognisance of any other consciousness than my own, and instead of intruding involuntarily into the world of other minds, was living continually in my own solitary future. Bertha was aware that I was greatly changed. To my surprise she had of late seemed to seek opportunities of remaining in my society, and had cultivated that kind of distant yet familiar talk which is customary between a husband and wife who live in polite and irrevocable alienation. I bore this with languid submission, and without feeling enough interest in her motives to be roused into keen observation; yet I could not help perceiving something triumphant and excited in her carriage and the expression of her face—something too subtle to express itself in words or tones, but giving one the idea that she lived in a state of expectation or hopeful suspense. My chief feeling was satisfaction that her inner self was once more shut out from me; and I almost revelled for the moment in the absent melancholy that made me answer her at cross purposes, and betray utter ignorance of what she had been saying. I remember well the look and the smile with which she one day said, after a mistake of this kind on my part: 'I used to think you were a clairvoyant, and that was the reason why you were so bitter against other clairvoyants, wanting to keep your monopoly; but I see now you have become rather duller than the rest of the world.'

I said nothing in reply. It occurred to me that her recent obtrusion of herself upon me might have been prompted by the wish to test my power of detecting some of her secrets; but I let the thought drop again at once: her motives and her deeds had no interest for me, and whatever pleasures she might be seeking, I had no wish to balk her. There was still pity in my soul for every living thing, and Bertha was living—was surrounded with possibilities of misery.

Just at this time there occurred an event which roused me somewhat from my inertia, and gave me an interest in the passing moment that I had thought impossible for me. It was a visit from Charles Meunier, who had written me word that he was coming to England for relaxation from too strenuous labour, and would like to see me. Meunier had now a European reputation; but his letter to me expressed that keen remembrance of an early regard, an early debt of sympathy, which is inseparable from nobility of character: and I too felt as if his presence would be to me like a transient resurrection into a happier pre-existence.

He came, and as far as possible, I renewed our old pleasure of making *tête-à-tête* excursions, though, instead of mountains and glaciers and the wide blue lake, we had to content ourselves with mere slopes and ponds and artificial plantations. The years had changed us both, but with what different result! Meunier was now a brilliant figure in society, to whom elegant women pretended to listen, and whose acquaintance was boasted of by noblemen ambitious of brains. He repressed with the utmost delicacy all betrayal of the shock which I am sure he must have received from our meeting, or of a desire to penetrate into my condition and circumstances, and sought by the utmost exertion of his charming social powers to make our reunion agreeable. Bertha was much struck by the unexpected fascinations of a visitor whom she had expected to find presentable only on the score of his celebrity, and put forth all her coquetries and accomplishments. Apparently she succeeded in attracting his admiration, for his manner towards her was attentive and flattering. The effect of his presence on me was so benignant, especially in those renewals of our old *tête-à-tête* wanderings, when he poured forth to me wonderful narratives of his professional experience, that more than once, when his talk turned on the psychological relations of disease, the thought crossed my mind that, if his stay with me were long enough, I might possibly bring myself to tell this man the secrets of my lot. Might there not lie some remedy for *me*, too, in his science? Might there not at least lie some comprehension and sympathy ready for me in his large and susceptible mind? But the thought only flickered feebly now and then, and died out before it could become a wish. The horror I had of again breaking in on the privacy of another soul, made me, by an irrational instinct, draw the shroud of concealment more closely around my own, as we automatically perform the gesture we feel to be wanting in another.

When Meunier's visit was approaching its conclusion, there happened an event which caused some excitement in our household, owing to the surprisingly strong effect it appeared to produce on Bertha—on Bertha, the self-possessed, who usually seemed inaccessible to feminine agitations, and did even her hate in a self-restrained hygienic manner. This event was the sudden severe illness of her maid, Mrs Archer. I have reserved to this moment the mention of a circumstance which had forced itself on my notice shortly before Meunier's arrival, namely, that there had been some quarrel between Bertha and this maid, apparently during a visit to a distant family, in which she had accompanied her mistress. I had overheard Archer speaking in a tone of bitter insolence, which I should have thought an adequate reason for immediate dismissal. No dismissal followed; on the contrary, Bertha seemed to be silently putting up with personal inconveniences from the exhibitions of this woman's temper. I was the more astonished to observe that her illness seemed a cause of strong solicitude to Bertha; that she was at the bedside night and day, and would allow no one else to officiate as head-nurse. It happened that our family doctor was out on a holiday, an accident which made Meunier's presence in the house doubly welcome, and he apparently entered into the case with an interest which seemed so much stronger than the ordinary professional feeling, that one day when he had fallen into a long fit of silence after visiting her, I said to him—

'Is this a very peculiar case of disease, Meunier?'

'No,' he answered, 'it is an attack of peritonitis,* which will be fatal, but which does not differ physically from many other cases that have come under my observation. But I'll tell you what I have on my mind. I want to make an experiment on this woman, if you will give me permission. It can do her no harm—will give her no pain—for I shall not make it until life is extinct to all purposes of sensation. I want to try the effect of transfusing blood into her arteries after the heart has ceased to beat for some minutes. I have tried the experiment again and again with animals that have died of this disease, with astounding results, and I want to try it on a human subject. I have the small tubes necessary, in a case I have with me, and the rest of the apparatus could be prepared readily. I should use my own blood—take it from my own arm. This woman won't live through the night, I'm convinced, and I want you to promise me your assistance in making the experiment. I can't do without another hand, but it would perhaps not be well to call in a medical assistant from among your provincial doctors. A disagreeable foolish version of the thing might get abroad.'

'Have you spoken to my wife on the subject?' I said, 'because she appears to be peculiarly sensitive about this woman: she has been a favourite maid.'

'To tell you the truth,' said Meunier, 'I don't want her to know about it. There are always insuperable difficulties with women in these matters, and the effect on the supposed dead body may be startling. You and I will sit up together, and be in readiness. When certain symptoms appear I shall take you in, and at the right moment we must manage to get every one else out of the room.'

I need not give our farther conversation on the subject. He entered very fully into the details, and overcame my repulsion from them, by exciting in me a mingled awe and curiosity concerning the possible results of his experiment.

We prepared everything, and he instructed me in my part as assistant. He had not told Bertha of his absolute conviction that Archer would not survive through the night, and endeavoured to persuade her to leave the patient and take a night's rest. But she was obstinate, suspecting the fact that death was at hand, and supposing that he wished merely to save her nerves. She refused to leave the sick-room. Meunier and I sat up together in the library, he making frequent visits to the sick-room, and returning with the information that the case was taking precisely the course he expected. Once he said to me, 'Can you imagine any cause of ill feeling this woman has against her mistress, who is so devoted to her?'

'I think there was some misunderstanding between them before her illness. Why do you ask?'

'Because I have observed for the last five or six hours—since, I fancy, she has lost all hope of recovery—there seems a strange prompting in her to say something which pain and failing strength forbid her to utter; and¯ there is a look of hideous meaning in her eyes, which she turns continually towards her mistress. In this disease the mind often remains singularly clear to the last.'

'I am not surprised at an indication of malevolent feeling in her,' I said. 'She is a woman who has always inspired me with distrust and dislike, but she managed to insinuate herself into her mistress's favour.' He was silent after this, looking at the fire with an air of absorption, till he went up-stairs again. He stayed away longer than usual, and on returning, said to me quietly, 'Come now.'

I followed him to the chamber where death was hovering. The dark hangings of the large bed made a background that gave a strong relief to Bertha's pale face as I entered. She started forward as she saw me enter, and then looked at Meunier with an expression of angry inquiry; but he lifted up his hand as if to impose silence, while he fixed his glance on the dying woman and felt her pulse. The face was pinched and ghastly, a cold perspiration was on the forehead, and the eyelids were lowered so as almost to conceal the large dark eyes. After a minute or two, Meunier walked round to the other side of the bed where Bertha stood, and with his usual air of gentle politeness towards her begged her to leave the patient under our care—everything should be done for her—she was no longer in a state to be conscious of an affectionate presence. Bertha was hesitating, apparently almost willing to believe his assurance and to comply. She looked round at the ghastly dying face, as if to read the confirmation of that assurance, when for a moment the lowered eyelids were raised again, and it seemed as if the eyes were looking towards Bertha, but blankly. A shudder passed through Bertha's frame, and she returned to her station near the pillow, tacitly implying that she would not leave the room.

The eyelids were lifted no more. Once I looked at Bertha as she watched the face of the dying one. She wore a rich *peignoir*,* and her blond hair was half covered by a lace cap: in her attire she was, as always, an elegant woman, fit to figure in a picture of modern aristocratic life: but I asked myself how that face of hers could ever

lack of feminine in Bertha

have seemed to me the face of a woman born of woman, with memories of childhood, capable of pain, needing to be fondled? The features at that moment seemed so preternaturally sharp, the eyes were so hard and eager—she looked like a cruel immortal, finding her spiritual feast in the agonies of a dying race. For across those hard features there came something like a flash when the last hour had been breathed out, and we all felt that the dark veil had completely fallen. What secret was there between Bertha and this woman? I turned my eyes from her with a horrible dread lest my insight should return, and I should be obliged to see what had been breeding about two unloving women's hearts. I felt that Bertha had been watching for the moment of death as the sealing of her secret: I thanked Heaven it could remain sealed for me.

Meunier said quietly, 'She is gone.' He then gave his arm to Bertha, and she submitted to be led out of the room.

I suppose it was at her order that two female attendants came into the room, and dismissed the younger one who had been present before. When they entered, Meunier had already opened the artery in the long thin neck that lay rigid on the pillow, and I dismissed them, ordering them to remain at a distance till we rang: the doctor, I said, had an operation to perform—he was not sure about the death. For the next twenty minutes I forgot everything but Meunier and the experiment in which he was so absorbed, that I think his senses would have been closed against all sounds or sights which had no relation to it. It was my task at first to keep up the artificial respiration in the body after the transfusion had been effected, but presently Meunier relieved me, and I could see the wondrous slow return of life; the breast began to heave, the inspirations became stronger, the eyelids quivered, and the soul seemed to have returned beneath them. The artificial respiration was withdrawn: still the breathing continued, and there was a movement of the lips.

Just then I heard the handle of the door moving: I suppose Bertha had heard from the women that they had been dismissed: probably a vague fear had arisen in her mind, for she entered with a look of alarm. She came to the foot of the bed and gave a stifled cry.

The dead woman's eyes were wide open, and met hers in full recognition—the recognition of hate. With a sudden strong effort,

the hand that Bertha had thought for ever still was pointed towards
her, and the haggard face moved. The gasping eager voice said—

'You mean to poison your husband . . . the poison is in the black
cabinet . . . I got it for you . . . you laughed at me, and told lies about
me behind my back, to make me disgusting . . . because you were
jealous . . . are you sorry . . . now?'

The lips continued to murmur, but the sounds were no longer
distinct. Soon there was no sound—only a slight movement: the
flame had leaped out, and was being extinguished the faster. The
wretched woman's heart-strings had been set to hatred and vengeance; the spirit of life had swept the chords for an instant, and was
gone again for ever. Great God! Is this what it is to live again* . . . to
wake up with our unstilled thirst upon us, with our unuttered curses
rising to our lips, with our muscles ready to act out their half-
committed sins?

Bertha stood pale at the foot of the bed, quivering and helpless,
despairing of devices, like a cunning animal whose hiding-places are
surrounded by swift-advancing flame. Even Meunier looked para-
lysed; life for that moment ceased to be a scientific problem to him.
As for me, this scene seemed of one texture with the rest of my
existence: horror was my familiar, and this new revelation was only
like an old pain recurring with new circumstances.

Since then Bertha and I have lived apart—she in her own neighbourhood, the mistress of half our wealth, I as a wanderer in foreign
countries, until I came to this Devonshire nest to die. Bertha lives
pitied and admired; for what had I against that charming woman,
whom every one but myself could have been happy with? There had
been no witness of the scene in the dying room except Meunier, and
while Meunier lived his lips were sealed by a promise to me.

Once or twice, weary of wandering, I rested in a favourite spot,
and my heart went out towards the men and women and children
whose faces were becoming familiar to me: but I was driven away
again in terror at the approach of my old insight—driven away to
live continually with the one Unknown Presence revealed and yet
hidden by the moving curtain of the earth and sky. Till at last disease
took hold of me and forced me to rest here—forced me to live
in dependence on my servants. And then the curse of insight—
of my double consciousness, came again, and has never left

me. I know all their narrow thoughts, their feeble regard, their half-wearied pity.

It is the 20th of September 1850. I know these figures I have just written, as if they were a long familiar inscription. I have seen them on this page in my desk unnumbered times, when the scene of my dying struggle has opened upon me. . . .

BROTHER JACOB

'Trompeurs, c'est pour vous que j'écris,
Attendez vous à la pareille'*

—La Fontaine

Mother's Guineas. The original frontispiece from *Cornhill Magazine*

The original illustrated initial from the *Cornhill* text

CHAPTER I

AMONG the many fatalities attending the bloom of young desire, that of blindly taking to the confectionery line has not, perhaps, been sufficiently considered. How is the son of a British yeoman,* who has been fed principally on salt pork and yeast dumplings, to know that there is satiety for the human stomach even in a paradise of glass jars full of sugared almonds and pink lozenges, and that the tedium of life can reach a pitch where plum-buns at discretion cease to offer the slightest enticement? Or how, at the tender age when a confectioner seems to him a very prince whom all the world must envy,—who breakfasts on macaroons, dines on marengs, sups on twelfth-cake,* and fills up the intermediate hours with sugar-candy or peppermint,—how is he to foresee the day of sad wisdom, when he will discern that the confectioner's calling is not socially influential, or favourable to a soaring ambition? I have known a man who turned out to have a metaphysical genius, incautiously, in the period of youthful buoyancy, commence his career as a dancing-master; and you may imagine the use that was made of this initial mistake by opponents who felt themselves bound to warn the public against his doctrine of the Inconceivable.* He could not give up his dancing-lessons, because he made his bread by them, and metaphysics would not have found him in so much as salt to his bread. It was really the same with Mr David Faux and the confectionery business. His uncle, the butler at the great house close by Brigford,* had made a pet of him in his early boyhood, and it was on a visit to this uncle that the confectioners' shops in that brilliant town had, on a single day, fired his tender imagination. He carried home the pleasing illusion that a confectioner must be at once the happiest and the foremost of men, since the things he made were not only the most beautiful to behold, but the very best eating, and such as the Lord Mayor must always order largely for his private recreation; so that when his father declared he must be put to a trade, David chose his line without a moment's hesitation; and, with a rashness inspired by a sweet tooth, wedded himself irrevocably to confectionery. Soon, however, the tooth lost its relish and fell into blank indifference; and all the while, his mind expanded, his ambition took new shapes, which could hardly be satisfied within the sphere his youthful ardour had chosen. But what was he to do? He was a young man of much mental activity, and, above all, gifted with a spirit of contrivance; but then, his faculties would not tell with great effect in any other medium than that of candied sugars, conserves, and pastry. Say what you will about the identity of the reasoning process in all branches of thought, or about the advantage of coming to subjects with a fresh mind, the adjustment of butter to flour, and of heat to pastry, is *not* the best preparation for the office of prime minister; besides, in the present imperfectly organized state of society, there are social barriers. David could invent delightful things in the way of drop-cakes, and he had the widest views of the sugar department; but in other directions he certainly felt hampered by the want of knowledge and practical skill; and the world is so inconveniently constituted, that the vague consciousness of being a fine fellow is no guarantee of success in any line of business.

This difficulty pressed with some severity on Mr David Faux, even before his apprenticeship was ended. His soul swelled with an impatient sense that he ought to become something very remarkable—that it was quite out of the question for him to put up with a narrow lot as other men did: he scorned the idea that he could accept an average. He was sure there was nothing average about him: even such a person as Mrs Tibbits, the washerwoman, perceived it, and probably had a preference for his linen. At that particular period he was weighing out gingerbread-nuts; but such an anomaly could not continue. No position could be suited to Mr David Faux that was not in the highest degree easy to the flesh and flattering to the spirit. If he had fallen on the present times, and enjoyed the advantages of a Mechanics' Institute,* he would certainly have taken to literature and have written reviews; but his education had not been liberal. He had read some novels from the adjoining circulating library, and had even bought the story of 'Inkle and Yarico',* which had made him feel very sorry for poor Mr Inkle; so that his ideas might not have been below a certain mark of the literary calling; but his spelling and diction were too unconventional.

When a man is not adequately appreciated or comfortably placed in his own country, his thoughts naturally turn towards foreign climes; and David's imagination circled round and round the utmost limits of his geographical knowledge, in search of a country where a young gentleman of pasty visage, lipless mouth, and stumpy hair, would be likely to be received with the hospitable enthusiasm which he had a right to expect. Having a general idea of America as a country where the population was chiefly black, it appeared to him the most propitious destination for an emigrant who, to begin with, had the broad and easily recognizable merit of whiteness; and this idea gradually took such strong possession of him that Satan seized the opportunity of suggesting to him that he might emigrate under easier circumstances, if he supplied himself with a little money from his master's till. But that evil spirit, whose understanding, I am convinced, has been much overrated, quite wasted his time on this occasion. David would certainly have liked well to have some of his master's money in his pocket, if he had been sure his master would have been the only man to suffer for it; but he was a cautious youth, and quite determined to run no risks on his own account. So he stayed out his apprenticeship, and committed no act of dishonesty that was at all likely to be discovered, reserving his plan of emigra- tion for a future opportunity. And the circumstances under which he carried it out were in this wise. Having been at home a week or two partaking of the family beans,* he had used his leisure in ascertaining a fact which was of considerable importance to him, namely, that his mother had a small sum in guineas painfully saved from her maiden perquisites, and kept in the corner of a drawer where her baby-linen had reposed for the last twenty years—ever since her son David had taken to his feet, with a slight promise of bow-legs which had not been altogether unfulfilled. Mr Faux, senior, had told his son very frankly, that he must not look to being set-up in business by *him*: with seven sons, and one of them a very healthy and well-developed idiot, who consumed a dumpling about eight inches in diameter every day, it was pretty well if they got a hundred apiece at his death. Under these circumstances, what was David to do? It was certainly hard that he should take his mother's money; but he saw no other ready means of getting any, and it was not to be expected that a young man of his merit should put up with inconviences that could be avoided. Besides, it is not robbery to take property belonging to your mother: she doesn't prosecute you. And David was very well behaved to his mother; he comforted her by speaking highly of him- self to her, and assuring her that he never fell into the vices he saw practised by other youths of his own age, and that he was particularly fond of honesty. If his mother would have given him her twenty guineas as a reward of this noble disposition, he really would not have stolen them from her, and it would have been more agreeable to his feelings. Nevertheless, to an active mind like David's, ingenuity is not without its pleasures: it was rather an interesting occupation to become stealthily acquainted with the wards of his mother's simple key (not in the least like Chubb's patent*), and to get one that would do its work equally well; and also to arrange a little drama by which he would escape suspicion, and run no risk of forfeiting the prospective hundred at his father's death, which would be convenient in the improbable case of his *not* making a large fortune in the 'Indies'.

First, he spoke freely of his intention to start shortly for Liverpool and take ship for America; a resolution which cost his good mother some pain, for, after Jacob the idiot, there was not one of her sons to whom her heart clung more than to her youngest-born, David. Next, it appeared to him that Sunday afternoon, when everybody was gone to church except Jacob and the cow-boy, was so singularly favourable an opportunity for sons who wanted to appropriate their mothers' guineas, that he half thought it must have been kindly intended by Providence for such purposes. Especially the third Sunday in Lent;* because Jacob had been out on one of his occasional wanderings for the last two days; and David, being a timid young man, had a considerable dread and hatred of Jacob, as of a large personage who went about habitually with a pitchfork in his hand.

Nothing could be easier, then, than for David on this Sunday afternoon to decline going to church, on the ground that he was going to tea at Mr Lunn's, whose pretty daughter Sally had been an early flame of his, and, when the church-goers were at a safe distance, to abstract the guineas from their wooden box and slip them into a small canvas bag—nothing easier than to call to the cow-boy that he was going, and tell him to keep an eye on the house for fear of Sunday tramps. David thought it would be easy, too, to get to a small thicket and bury his bag in a hole he had already made and covered up under the roots of an old hollow ash, and he had, in fact, found the hole without a moment's difficulty, had uncovered it, and was about gently to drop the bag into it, when the sound of a large body rustling towards him with something like a bellow was such a surprise to David, who, as a gentleman gifted with much contrivance, was naturally only prepared for what he expected, that instead of dropping the bag gently he let it fall so as to make it untwist and vomit forth the shining guineas. In the same moment he looked up and saw his dear brother Jacob close upon him, holding the pitchfork so that the bright smooth prongs were a yard in advance of his own body, and about a foot off David's. (A learned friend, to whom I once narrated this history, observed that it was David's guilt which made these prongs formidable, and that the *mens nil conscia sibi** strips a pitchfork of all terrors. I thought this idea so valuable, that I obtained his leave to use it on condition of suppressing his name.) Nevertheless, David did not entirely lose his presence of mind; for in that case he would have sunk on the earth or started backward; whereas he kept his ground and smiled at Jacob, who nodded his head up and down, and said, 'Hoich, Zavy!' in a painfully equivocal manner. David's heart was beating audibly, and if he had had any lips they would have been pale; but his mental activity, instead of being paralyzed, was stimulated. While he was inwardly praying (he always prayed when he was much frightened),—'Oh, save me this once, and I'll never get into danger again!'—he was thrusting his hand into his pocket in search of a box of yellow lozenges, which he had brought with him from Brigford among other delicacies of the same portable kind, as a means of conciliating proud beauty, and more particularly the beauty of Miss Sarah Lunn. Not one of these delicacies had he ever offered to poor Jacob, for David was not a young man to waste his jujubes and barley-sugar in giving pleasure to people from whom he expected nothing. But an idiot with equivocal intentions and a pitchfork is as well worth flattering and cajoling as if he were Louis Napoleon.* So David, with a promptitude equal to the occasion, drew out his box of yellow lozenges, lifted the lid, and performed a pantomime with his mouth and fingers, which was meant to imply that he was delighted to see his dear brother Jacob, and seized the opportunity of making him a small present, which he would find particularly agreeable to the taste. Jacob, you understand, was not an intense idiot, but within a certain limited range knew how to choose the good and reject the evil: he took one lozenge, by way of test, and sucked it as if he had been a philosopher; then, in as great an ecstacy at its new and complex savour as Caliban at the taste of Trinculo's wine,* chuckled and stroked this suddenly beneficent brother, and held out his hand for more; for, except in fits of anger,

Jacob was not ferocious or needlessly predatory. David's courage half returned, and he left off praying; pouring a dozen lozenges into Jacob's palm, and trying to look very fond of him. He congratulated himself that he had formed the plan of going to see Miss Sally Lunn* this afternoon, and that, as a consequence, he had brought with him these propitiatory delicacies: he was certainly a lucky fellow; indeed, it was always likely Providence should be fonder of him than of other apprentices, and since he *was* to be interrupted, why, an idiot was preferable to any other sort of witness. For the first time in his life, David thought he saw the advantage of idiots.

As for Jacob, he had thrust his pitchfork into the ground, and had thrown himself down beside it, in thorough abandonment to the unprecedented pleasure of having five lozenges in his mouth at once, blinking meanwhile, and making inarticulate sounds of gustative content. He had not yet given any sign of noticing the guineas, but in seating himself he had laid his broad right hand on them, and unconsciously kept it in that position, absorbed in the sensations of his palate. If he could only be kept so occupied with the lozenges as not to see the guineas before David could manage to cover them! That was David's best hope of safety; for Jacob knew his mother's guineas; it had been part of their common experience as boys to be allowed to look at these handsome coins, and rattle them in their box on high days and holidays, and among all Jacob's narrow experiences as to money, this was likely to be the most memorable.

'Here, Jacob,' said David, in an insinuating tone, handing the box to him, 'I'll give 'em all to you. Run!—make haste!—else somebody'll come and take 'em.'

David, not having studied the psychology of idiots,* was not aware that they are not to be wrought upon by imaginative fears. Jacob took the box with his left hand, but saw no necessity for running away. Was ever a promising young man wishing to lay the foundation of his fortune by appropriating his mother's guineas obstructed by such a day-mare as this? But the moment must come when Jacob would move his right hand to draw off the lid of the tin box, and then David would sweep the guineas into the hole with the utmost address and swiftness, and immediately seat himself upon them. Ah, no! It's of no use to have foresight when you are dealing with an idiot: he is not to be calculated upon. Jacob's right hand was given to vague clutching and throwing; it suddenly clutched the guineas as if they had been so many pebbles, and was raised in an attitude which promised to scatter them like seed over a distant bramble, when, from some prompting or other—probably of an unwonted sensation—it paused, descended to Jacob's knee, and opened slowly under the inspection of Jacob's dull eyes. David began to pray again, but immediately desisted—another resource having occurred to him.

'Mother! zinnies!' exclaimed the innocent Jacob. Then, looking at David, he said, interrogatively, 'Box?'

'Hush! hush!' said David, summoning all his ingenuity in this severe strait. 'See, Jacob!' He took the tin box from his brother's hand, and emptied it of the lozenges, returning half of them to Jacob, but secretly keeping the rest in his own hand. Then he held out the empty box, and said, 'Here's the box, Jacob! The box for the guineas!' gently sweeping them from Jacob's palm into the box.

This procedure was not objectionable to Jacob; on the contrary, the guineas clinked so pleasantly as they fell, that he wished for a repetition of the sound, and seizing the box, began to rattle it very gleefully. David, seizing the opportunity, deposited his reserve of lozenges in the ground and hastily swept some earth over them. 'Look, Jacob!' he said, at last. Jacob paused from his clinking, and looked into the hole, while David began to scratch away the earth, as if in doubtful expectation. When the lozenges were laid bare, he took them out one by one, and gave them to Jacob.

'Hush!' he said, in a loud whisper, 'Tell nobody—all for Jacob—hush—sh—sh! Put guineas in the hole—they'll come out like this!' To make the lesson more complete, he took a guinea, and lowering it into the hole, said, 'Put in *so*.' Then, as he took the last lozenge out, he said, 'Come out *so*,' and put the lozenge into Jacob's hospitable mouth.

Jacob turned his head on one side, looked first at his brother and then at the hole, like a reflective monkey, and, finally, laid the box of guineas in the hole with much decision. David made haste to add every one of the stray coins, put on the lid, and covered it well with earth, saying in his most coaxing tone—

'Take 'm out to-morrow, Jacob; all for Jacob! Hush—sh—sh!'

Jacob, to whom this once indifferent brother had all at once become a sort of sweet-tasted fetish, stroked David's best coat with his adhesive fingers, and then hugged him with an accompaniment of that mingled chuckling and gurgling by which he was accustomed to express the milder passions. But if he had chosen to bite a small morsel out of his beneficent brother's cheek, David would have been obliged to bear it.

And here I must pause, to point out to you the short-sightedness of human contrivance. This ingenious young man, Mr David Faux, thought he had achieved a triumph of cunning when he had associated himself in his brother's rudimentary mind with the flavour of yellow lozenges. But he had yet to learn that it is a dreadful thing to make an idiot fond of you, when you yourself are not of an affectionate disposition: especially an idiot with a pitchfork—obviously a difficult friend to shake off by rough usage.

It may seem to you rather a blundering contrivance for a clever young man to bury the guineas. But, if everything had turned out as David had calculated, you would have seen that his plan was worthy of his talents. The guineas would have lain safely in the earth while the theft was discovered, and David, with the calm of conscious innocence, would have lingered at home, reluctant to say good-bye to his dear mother while she was in grief about her guineas; till at length, on the eve of his departure, he would have disinterred them in the strictest privacy, and carried them on his own person without inconvenience. But David, you perceive, had reckoned without his host, or, to speak more precisely, without his idiot brother—an item of so uncertain and fluctuating a character, that I doubt whether he would not have puzzled the astute heroes of M. de Balzac*, whose foresight is so remarkably at home in the future.

It was clear to David now that he had only one alternative before him: he must either renounce the guineas, by quietly putting them back in his mother's drawer (a course not unattended with difficulty); or he must leave more than a suspicion behind him, by departing early the next morning without giving notice, and with the guineas in his pocket. For if he gave notice that he was going, his mother, he knew, would insist on fetching from her box of guineas the three she had always promised him as his share; indeed, in his original plan, he had counted on this as a means by which the theft would be discovered under circumstances that would themselves speak for his innocence; but now, as I need hardly explain, that well-combined plan was completely frustrated. Even if David could have bribed Jacob with perpetual lozenges, an idiot's secrecy is itself betrayal. He dared not even go to tea at Mr Lunn's, for in that case he would have lost sight of Jacob, who, in his impatience for the crop of lozenges, might scratch up the box again while he was absent, and carry it home—depriving him at once of reputation and guineas. No! he must think of nothing all the rest of this day, but of coaxing Jacob and keeping him out of mischief. It was a fatiguing and anxious evening to David; nevertheless, he dared not go to sleep without tying a piece of string to his thumb and great toe, to secure his frequent waking; for he meant to be up with the first peep of dawn, and be far out of reach before breakfast-time. His father, he thought, would certainly cut him off with a shilling; but what then? Such a striking young man as he would be sure to be well received in the West Indies: in foreign countries there are always openings—even for cats.* It was probable that some Princess Yarico would want him to marry her, and make him presents of very large jewels beforehand; after which, he needn't marry her unless he liked. David had made up his mind not to steal any more, even from people who were fond of him: it was an unpleasant way of making your fortune in a world where you were likely to be surprised in the act by brothers. Such alarms did not agree with David's constitution, and he had felt so much nausea this evening that no doubt his liver was affected. Besides, he would have been greatly hurt not to be thought well of in the world: he always meant to make a figure, and be thought worthy of the best seats and the best morsels.

Ruminating to this effect on the brilliant future in reserve for him, David by the help of his check-string kept himself on the alert to seize the time of earliest dawn for his rising and departure. His brothers, of course, were early risers, but he should anticipate them by at least an hour and a half, and the little room which he had to himself as only an occasional visitor, had its window over the horse-block,* so that he could slip out through the window without the least difficulty. Jacob, the horrible Jacob, had an awkward trick of getting up before everybody else, to stem his hunger by emptying the milk-bowl that was 'duly set' for him; but of late he had taken to sleeping in the hay-loft, and if he came into the house, it would be on the opposite side to that from which David was making his exit. There was no need to think of Jacob; yet David was liberal enough to bestow a curse on him—it was the only thing he ever did bestow gratuitously. His small bundle of clothes was ready packed, and he was soon treading lightly on the steps of the horse-block, soon walking at a smart pace across the fields towards the thicket. It would take him no more than two minutes to get out the box; he could make out the tree it was under by the pale strip where the bark was off, although the dawning light was rather dimmer in the thicket. But what, in the name of—burnt pastry—was that large body with a staff planted beside it, close at the foot of the ash-tree? David paused, not to make up his mind as to the nature of the apparition—he had not the happiness of doubting for a moment that the staff was Jacob's pitchfork—but to gather the self-command necessary for addressing his brother with a sufficiently honeyed accent. Jacob was absorbed in scratching up the earth, and had not heard David's approach.

'I say, Jacob,' said David in a loud whisper, just as the tin box was lifted out of the hole.

Jacob looked up, and discerning his sweet-flavoured brother, nodded and grinned in the dim light in a way that made him seem to David like a triumphant demon. If he had been of an impetuous disposition, he would have snatched the pitchfork from the ground and impaled this fraternal demon. But David was by no means impetuous; he was a young man greatly given to calculate consequences, a habit which has been held to be the foundation of virtue. But somehow it had not precisely that effect in David: he calculated whether an action would harm himself, or whether it would only harm other people. In the former case he was very timid about satisfying his immediate desires, but in the latter he would risk the result with much courage.

'Give it *me*, Jacob,' he said, stooping down and patting his brother, 'Let us see.'

Jacob, finding the lid rather tight, gave the box to his brother in perfect faith. David raised the lid, and shook his head, while Jacob put his finger in and took out a guinea to taste whether the metamorphosis into lozenges was complete and satisfactory.

'No, Jacob; too soon, too soon,' said David, when the guinea had been tasted. 'Give it me; we'll go and bury it somewhere else; we'll put it in yonder,' he added, pointing vaguely toward the distance.

David screwed on the lid, while Jacob, looking grave, rose and grasped his pitchfork. Then, seeing David's bundle, he snatched it, like a too officious Newfoundland, stuck his pitchfork into it and carried it over his shoulder in triumph as he accompanied David and the box out of the thicket.

What on earth was David to do? It would have been easy to frown at Jacob, and kick him, and order him to get away; but David dared as soon have kicked the bull. Jacob was quiet as long as he was treated indulgently; but on the slightest show of anger, he became unmanageable, and was liable to fits of fury which would have made him formidable even without his pitchfork. There was no mastery to be obtained over him except by kindness or guile. David tried guile.

'Go, Jacob,' he said, when they were out of the thicket—pointing towards the house as he spoke; 'go and fetch me a spade—a spade. But give *me* the bundle,' he added, trying to reach it from the fork, where it hung high above Jacob's tall shoulder.

But Jacob showed as much alacrity in obeying as a wasp shows in leaving a sugar-basin. Near David, he felt himself in the vicinity of lozenges: he chuckled and rubbed his brother's back, brandishing the bundle higher out of reach. David, with an inward groan, changed his tactics, and walked on as fast as he could. It was not safe to linger. Jacob would get tired of following him, or, at all events, could be eluded. If they could once get to the distant highroad, a coach would overtake them, David would mount it, having previously by some ingenious means secured his bundle, and then Jacob might howl and flourish his pitchfork as much as he liked. Meanwhile he was under the fatal necessity of being very kind to this ogre, and of providing a large breakfast for him when they stopped at a roadside inn. It was already three hours since they had started, and David was tired. Would no coach be coming up soon? he inquired. No coach for the next two hours. But there was a carrier's cart to come immediately, on its way to the next town. If he could slip out, even leaving his bundle behind, and get into the cart without Jacob! But there was a new obstacle. Jacob had recently discovered a remnant of sugar-candy in one of his brother's tailpockets; and, since then, had cautiously kept his hold on that limb of the garment, perhaps with an expectation that there would be a further development of sugar-candy after a longer or shorter interval. Now every one who has worn a coat will understand the sensibilities that must keep a man from starting away in a hurry when there is a grasp on his coat-tail. David looked forward to being well received among strangers, but it might make a difference if he had only one tail to his coat.

He felt himself in a cold perspiration. He could walk no more: he must get into the cart and let Jacob get in with him. Presently a cheering idea occurred to him: after so large a breakfast, Jacob would be sure to go to sleep in the cart; you see at once that David meant to seize his bundle, jump out, and be free. His expectation was partly fulfilled: Jacob did go to sleep in the cart, but it was in a peculiar attitude—it was with his arms tightly fastened round his dear brother's body; and if ever David attempted to move, the grasp tightened with the force of an affectionate boa-constrictor.

'Th' innicent's fond on you,' observed the carrier, thinking that David was probably an amiable brother, and wishing to pay him a compliment.

David groaned. The ways of thieving were not ways of pleasant-ness.* Oh, why had he an idiot brother? Or why, in general, was the world so constituted that a man could not take his mother's guineas comfortably? David became grimly speculative.

Copious dinner at noon for Jacob; but little dinner, because little appetite, for David. Instead of eating, he plied Jacob with beer; for through this liberality he descried a hope. Jacob fell into a dead sleep, at last, *without* having his arms round David, who paid the reckon-ing, took his bundle, and walked off. In another half-hour he was on the coach on his way to Liverpool, smiling the smile of the triumph-ant wicked. He was rid of Jacob—he was bound for the Indies, where a gullible princess awaited him. He would never steal any more, but there would be no need; he would show himself so deserving, that people would make him presents freely. He must give up the notion of his father's legacy; but it was not likely he would ever want that trifle; and even if he did—why, it was a compensation to think that in being for ever divided from his family he was divided from Jacob, more terrible than Gorgon or Demogorgon* to David's timid green eyes. Thank heaven he should never see Jacob any more!

CHAPTER II

IT was nearly six years after the departure of Mr David Faux for the West Indies, that the vacant shop in the market-place at Grimworth was understood to have been let to the stranger with a sallow complexion and a buff cravat, whose first appearance had caused some excitement in the bar of the Woolpack, where he had called to wait for the coach.

Grimworth, to a discerning eye, was a good place to set up shop-keeping in. There was no competition in it at present; the Church-people had their own grocer and draper; the Dissenters* had theirs; and the two or three butchers found a ready market for their joints without strict reference to religious persuasion—except that the rector's wife had given a general order for the veal sweet-breads and the mutton kidneys, while Mr Rodd, the Baptist minister, had requested that, so far as was compatible with the fair accommodation of other customers, the sheep's trotters might be reserved for him. And it was likely to be a growing place, for the trustees of Mr Zephaniah Crypt's Charity, under the stimulus of a late visitation by commissioners,* were beginning to apply long-accumulating funds to the rebuilding of the Yellow Coat School,* which was henceforth to be carried forward on a greatly-extended scale, the testator having left no restrictions concerning the curriculum, but only concerning the coat.

The shopkeepers at Grimworth were by no means unanimous as to the advantages promised by this prospect of increased population and trading, being substantial men, who liked doing a quiet business in which they were sure of their customers, and could calculate their returns to a nicety. Hitherto, it had been held a point of honour by the families in Grimworth parish, to buy their sugar and their flannel at the shops where their fathers and mothers had bought before them; but, if new-comers were to bring in the system of neck-and-neck trading, and solicit feminine eyes by gown-pieces laid in fan-like folds, and surmounted by artificial flowers, giving them a factitious charm (for on what human figure would a gown sit like a fan, or what female head was like a bunch of China-asters?*), or, if new grocers were to fill their windows with mountains of currants and sugar, made seductive by contrast and tickets,—what security was there for Grimworth, that a vagrant spirit in shopping, once introduced, would not in the end carry the most important families to the larger market town of Cattleton, where, business being done on a system of small profits and quick returns, the fashions were of the freshest, and goods of all kinds might be bought at an advantage?

With this view of the times predominant among the tradespeople at Grimworth, their uncertainty concerning the nature of the business which the sallow-complexioned stranger was about to set up in the vacant shop, naturally gave some additional strength to the fears of the less sanguine. If he was going to sell drapery, it was probable that a pale-faced fellow like that would deal in showy and inferior articles—printed cottons and muslins which would leave their dye in the wash-tub, jobbed linen* full of knots, and flannel that would soon look like gauze. If grocery, then it was to be hoped that no mother of a family would trust the teas of an untried grocer. Such things had been known in some parishes as tradesmen going about canvassing for custom with cards in their pockets: when people came from nobody knew where, there was no knowing what they might do. It was a thousand pities that Mr Moffat, the auctioneer and broker, had died without leaving anybody to follow him in the business, and Mrs Cleve's trustee ought to have known better than to let a shop to a stranger. Even the discovery that ovens were being put up on the premises, and that the shop was, in fact, being fitted up for a confectioner and pastry-cook's business, hitherto unknown in Grimworth, did not quite suffice to turn the scale in the new-comer's favour, though the landlady at the Woolpack defended him warmly, said he seemed to be a very clever young man, and from what she could make out, came of a very good family; indeed, was most likely a good many people's betters.

It certainly made a blaze of light and colour, almost as if a rainbow had suddenly descended into the market-place, when, one fine morning, the shutters were taken down* from the new shop, and the two windows displayed their decorations. On one side, there were the variegated tints of collared and marbled meats,* set off by bright green leaves, the pale brown of glazed pies, the rich tones of sauces and bottled fruits enclosed in their veil of glass—altogether a sight to bring tears into the eyes of a Dutch painter;* and on the other, there was a predominance of the more delicate hues of pink, and white, and yellow, and buff, in the abundant lozenges, candies, sweet biscuits and icings, which to the eyes of a bilious person might easily have been blended into a faëry landscape in Turner's latest style.* What a sight to dawn upon the eyes of Grimworth children! They almost forgot to go to their dinner that day, their appetites being preoccupied with imaginary sugar-plums; and I think even Punch, setting up his tabernacle in the market-place,* would not have succeeded in drawing them away from those shop-windows, where they stood according to gradations of size and strength, the biggest and strongest being nearest the window, and the little ones in the outermost rows lifting wide-open eyes and mouths towards the upper tier of jars, like small birds at meal-time.

The elder inhabitants pished and pshawed a little at the folly of the new shopkeeper in venturing on such an outlay in goods that would not keep; to be sure, Christmas was coming, but what housewife in Grimworth would not think shame to furnish forth her table with articles that were not home-cooked? No, no. Mr Edward Freely, as he called himself, was deceived, if he thought Grimworth money was to flow into his pockets on such terms.

Edward Freely was the name that shone in gilt letters on a mazarine* ground over the doorplace of the new shop—a generous-sounding name, that might have belonged to the open-hearted, improvident hero of an old comedy, who would have delighted in raining sugared almonds, like a new manna-gift,* among that small generation outside the windows. But Mr Edward Freely was a man whose impulses were kept in due subordination: he held that the desire for sweets and pastry must only be satisfied in a direct ratio with the power of paying for them. If the smallest child in Grimworth would go to him with a halfpenny in its tiny fist, he would, after ringing the halfpenny, deliver a just equivalent in 'rock'. He was not a man to cheat even the smallest child—he often said so, observing at the same time that he loved honesty, and also that he was very tender-hearted, though he didn't show his feelings as some people did.

Either in reward of such virtue, or according to some more hidden law of sequence,* Mr Freely's business, in spite of prejudice, started under favourable auspices. For Mrs Chaloner, the rector's wife, was among the earliest customers at the shop, thinking it only right to encourage a new parishioner who had made a decorous appearance at church; and she found Mr Freely a most civil, obliging young man, and intelligent to a surprising degree for a confectioner; well-principled, too, for in giving her useful hints about choosing sugars he had thrown much light on the dishonesty of other tradesmen. Moreover, he had been in the West Indies, and had seen the very estate which had been her poor grandfather's property; and he said the missionaries were the only cause of the negro's discontent—an observing young man, evidently. Mrs Chaloner ordered wine-biscuits and olives, and gave Mr Freely to understand that she should find his shop a great convenience. So did the doctor's wife, and so did Mrs Gate, at the large carding mill,* who, having high connections frequently visiting her, might be expected to have a large consumption of ratafias* and macaroons.

The less aristocratic matrons of Grimworth seemed likely at first to justify their husbands' confidence that they would never pay a percentage of profits on drop-cakes, instead of making their own, or get up a hollow show of liberal housekeeping by purchasing slices of collared meat when a neighbour came in for supper. But it is my task to narrate the gradual corruption of Grimworth manners from their primitive simplicity—a melancholy task, if it were not cheered by the prospect of the fine peripateia* or downfall by which the progress of the corruption was ultimately checked.

It was young Mrs Steene, the veterinary surgeon's wife, who first gave way to temptation. I fear she had been rather over-educated for her station in life, for she knew by heart many passages in 'Lalla Rookh', the 'Corsair', and the 'Siege of Corinth',* which had given her a distaste for domestic occupations, and caused her a withering disappointment at the discovery that Mr Steene, since his marriage, had lost all interest in the 'bulbul',* openly preferred discussing the nature of spavin* with a coarse neighbour, and was angry if the pudding turned out watery—indeed, was simply a top-booted 'vet.', who came in hungry at dinner-time; and not in the least like a nobleman turned Corsair out of pure scorn for his race, or like a renegade* with a turban and crescent, unless it were in the irritability of his temper. And scorn is such a very different thing in top-boots!

This brutal man had invited a supper-party for Christmas eve, when he would expect to see mince-pies on the table. Mrs Steene had prepared her mince-meat, and had devoted much butter, fine flour, and labour, to the making of a batch of pies in the morning; but they proved to be so very heavy when they came out of the oven, that she could only think with trembling of the moment when her husband should catch sight of them on the supper-table. He would storm at her, she was certain; and before all the company; and then she should never help crying: it was so dreadful to think she had come to that, after the bulbul and everything! Suddenly the thought darted through her mind that *this once* she might send for a dish of mince-pies from Freely's: she knew he had some. But what was to become of the eighteen heavy mince-pies? Oh, it was of no use thinking about that; it was very expensive—indeed, making mince-pies at all was a great expense, when they were not sure to turn out well: it would be much better to buy them ready-made. You paid a little more for them, but there was no risk of waste.

Such was the sophistry with which this misguided young woman—enough. Mrs Steene sent for the mince-pies, and, I am grieved to add, garbled her household accounts in order to conceal the fact from her husband. This was the second step in a downward course, all owing to a young woman's being out of harmony with her circumstances, yearning after renegades and bulbuls, and being subject to claims from a veterinary surgeon fond of mince-pies. The third step was to harden herself by telling the fact of the bought mince-pies to her intimate friend Mrs Mole, who had already guessed it, and who subsequently encouraged herself in buying a mould of jelly, instead of exerting her own skill, by the reflection that 'other people' did the same sort of thing. The infection spread; soon there was a party or clique in Grimworth on the side of 'buying at Freely's'; and many husbands, kept for some time in the dark on this point, innocently swallowed at two mouthfuls a tart on which they were paying a profit of a hundred per cent, and as innocently encouraged a fatal disingenuousness in the partners of their bosoms by praising the pastry. Others, more keen-sighted, winked at the too frequent presentation on washing-days, and at impromptu suppers, of superior spiced-beef, which flattered their palates more than the cold remnants they had formerly been contented with. Every housewife who had once 'bought at Freely's' felt a secret joy when she detected a similar perversion in her neighbour's practice, and soon only two or three old-fashioned mistresses of families held out in the protest against the growing demoralization, saying to their neighbours who came to sup with them, 'I can't offer you Freely's beef, or Freely's cheese-cakes; everything in our house is home-made; I'm afraid you'll hardly have any appetite for our plain pastry.' The doctor, whose cook was not satisfactory, the curate, who kept no cook, and the mining agent, who was a great *bon vivant*, even began to rely on Freely for the greater part of their dinner, when they wished to give an entertainment of some brilliancy. In short, the business of manufacturing the more fanciful viands was fast passing out of the hands of maids and matrons in private families, and was becoming the work of a special commercial organ.

I am not ignorant that this sort of thing is called the inevitable course of civilization, division of labour,* and so forth, and that the maids and matrons may be said to have had their hands set free from cookery to add to the wealth of society in some other way. Only it happened at Grimworth, which, to be sure, was a low place, that the maids and matrons could do nothing with their hands at all better than cooking; not even those who had always made heavy cakes and leathery pastry. And so it came to pass, that the progress of civilization at Grimworth was not otherwise apparent than in the impoverishment of men, the gossiping idleness of women, and the heightening prosperity of Mr Edward Freely.

The Yellow Coat School was a double source of profit to the calculating confectioner; for he opened an eating-room for the superior workmen employed on the new school, and he accommodated the pupils at the old school by giving great attention to the fancy-sugar department. When I think of the sweet-tasted swans and other ingenious white shapes crunched by the small teeth of that rising generation, I am glad to remember that a certain amount of calcareous* food has been held good for young creatures whose bones are not quite formed; for I have observed these delicacies to have an inorganic flavour which would have recommended them greatly to that young lady of the 'Spectator's' acquaintance* who habitually made her dessert on the stems of tobacco-pipes.

As for the confectioner himself, he made his way gradually into Grimworth homes, as his commodities did, in spite of some initial repugnance. Somehow or other, his reception as a guest seemed a thing that required justifying, like the purchasing of his pastry. In the first place, he was a stranger, and therefore open to suspicion; secondly, the confectionery business was so entirely new at Grimworth, that its place in the scale of rank had not been distinctly ascertained. There was no doubt about drapers and grocers, when they came of good old Grimworth families, like Mr Luff and Mr Prettyman: they visited with the Palfreys,* who farmed their own land, played many a game at whist with the doctor, and condescended a little towards the timber-merchant, who had lately taken to the coal-trade also, and had got new furniture; but whether a confectioner should be admitted to this higher level of respectability, or should be understood to find his associates among butchers and bakers, was a new question on which tradition threw no light. His being a bachelor was in his favour, and would perhaps have been enough to turn the scale, even if Mr Edward Freely's other personal pretensions had been of an entirely insignificant cast. But so far from this, it very soon appeared that he was a remarkable young man, who had been in the West Indies, and had seen many wonders by sea and land, so that he could charm the ears of Grimworth Desdemonas* with stories of strange fishes, especially sharks, which he had stabbed in the nick of time by bravely plunging overboard just as the monster was turning on his side to devour the cook's mate; of terrible fevers which he had undergone in a land where the wind blows from all quarters at once; of rounds of toast cut straight from the bread-fruit trees; of toes bitten off by land-crabs; of large honours that had been offered to him as a man who knew what was what, and was therefore particularly needed in a tropical climate; and of a Creole heiress who had wept bitterly at his departure. Such conversational talents as these, we know, will overcome disadvantages of complexion; and young Towers, whose cheeks were of the finest pink, set off by a fringe of dark whisker, was quite eclipsed by the presence of the sallow Mr Freely. So exceptional a confectioner elevated his business, and might well begin to make disengaged hearts flutter a little.

Fathers and mothers were naturally more slow and cautious in their recognition of the new-comer's merits.

'He's an amusing fellow,' said Mr Prettyman, the highly respectable grocer. (Mrs Prettyman was a Miss Fothergill, and her sister had married a London mercer.*) 'He's an amusing fellow; and I've no objection to his making one at the Oyster Club; but he's a bit too fond of riding the high horse. He's uncommonly knowing, I'll allow; but how came he to go to the Indies? I should like that answered. It's unnatural in a confectioner. I'm not fond of people that have been beyond seas, if they can't give a good account how they happened to go. When folks go so far off, it's because they've got little credit nearer home—that's my opinion. However, he's got some good rum; but I don't want to be hand and glove with him, for all that.'

It was this kind of dim suspicion which beclouded the view of Mr Freely's qualities in the maturer minds of Grimworth through the early months of his residence there. But when the confectioner ceased to be a novelty, the suspicions also ceased to be novel, and people got tired of hinting at them, especially as they seemed to be refuted by his advancing prosperity and importance. Mr Freely was becoming a person of influence in the parish; he was found useful as an overseer of the poor,* having great firmness in enduring other people's pain, which firmness, he said, was due to his great benevolence; he always did what was good for people in the end. Mr Chaloner had even selected him as clergyman's churchwarden, for he was a very handy man, and much more of Mr Chaloner's opinion in everything about church business than the older parishioners. Mr Freely was a very regular churchman, but at the Oyster Club he was sometimes a little free in his conversation, more than hinting at a life of Sultanic self-indulgence which he had passed in the West Indies, shaking his head now and then and smiling rather bitterly, as men are wont to do when they intimate that they have become a little too wise to be instructed about a world which has long been flat and stale to them.*

For some time, he was quite general in his attentions to the fair sex, combining the gallantries of a lady's man with a severity of criticism on the person and manners of absent belles, which tended rather to stimulate in the feminine breast the desire to conquer the approval of so fastidious a judge. Nothing short of the very best in the department of female charms and virtues could suffice to kindle the ardour of Mr Edward Freely, who had become familiar with the most luxuriant and dazzling beauty in the West Indies. It may seem incredible that a confectioner should have ideas and conversation so much resembling those to be met with in a higher walk of life, but it must be remembered that he had not merely travelled, he had also bow-legs and a sallow, small-featured visage, so that nature herself had stamped him for a fastidious connoisseur of the fair sex.

At last, however, it seemed clear that Cupid had found a sharper arrow than usual, and that Mr Freely's heart was pierced. It was the general talk among the young people at Grimworth. But was it really love? and not rather ambition? Miss Fullilove, the timber-merchant's daughter, was quite sure that if *she* were Miss Penny Palfrey, she would be cautious; it was not a good sign, when men looked so much above themselves for a wife. For it was no less a person than Miss Penelope Palfrey, second daughter of the Mr Palfrey who farmed his own land, that had attracted Mr Freely's peculiar regard, and conquered his fastidiousness; and no wonder; for the Ideal, as exhibited in the finest waxwork, was perhaps never so closely approached by the Real* as in the person of the pretty Penelope. Her yellowish flaxen hair did not curl naturally, I admit, but its bright crisp ringlets were such smooth, perfect miniature tubes, that you would have longed to pass your little finger through them, and feel their soft elasticity. She wore them in a crop,* for in those days, when society was in a healthier state, young ladies wore crops long after they were twenty, and Penelope was not yet nineteen. Like the waxen ideal, she had round blue eyes, and round nostrils in her little nose, and teeth such as the ideal would be seen to have, if it ever showed them. Altogether, she was a small, round thing, as neat as a pink and white double daisy, and as guileless; for I hope it does not argue guile in a pretty damsel of nineteen, to think that she should like to have a beau and be 'engaged', when her elder sister had already been in that position a year and a half. To be sure, there was young Towers always coming to the house; but Penny felt convinced he only came to see her brother, for he never had anything to say to her, and never offered her his arm, and was as awkward and silent as possible.

It is not unlikely that Mr Freely had early been smitten by Penny's charms, as brought under his observation at church, but he had to make his way in society a little before he could come into nearer contact with them; and even after he was well received in Grimworth families, it was a long while before he could converse with Penny otherwise than in an incidental meeting at Mr Luff's. It was not so easy to get invited to Long Meadows, the residence of the Palfreys; for though Mr Palfrey had been losing money of late years, not being able quite to recover his feet after the terrible murrain* which forced him to borrow, his family were far from considering themselves on the same level even as the old-established tradespeople with whom they visited. The greatest people, even kings and queens, must visit with somebody, and the equals of the great are scarce. They were especially scarce at Grimworth, which, as I have before observed, was a low parish, mentioned with the most scornful brevity in gazetteers. Even the great people there were far behind those of their own standing in other parts of this realm. Mr Palfrey's farmyard doors had the paint all worn off them, and the front garden walks had long been merged in a general weediness. Still, his father had been called Squire Palfrey, and had been respected by the last Grimworth generation as a man who could afford to drink too much in his own house.

Pretty Penny was not blind to the fact that Mr Freely admired her, and she felt sure that it was he who had sent her a beautiful valentine; but her sister seemed to think so lightly of him (all young ladies think lightly of the gentlemen to whom they are not engaged), that Penny never dared mention him, and trembled and blushed whenever they met him, thinking of the valentine, which was very strong in its expressions, and which she felt guilty of knowing by heart. A man who had been to the Indies, and knew the sea so well, seemed to her a sort of public character, almost like Robinson Crusoe or Captain Cook;* and Penny had always wished her husband to be a remarkable personage, likely to be put in Mangnall's Questions,* with which register of the immortals she had become acquainted during her one year at a boarding-school. Only it seemed strange that a remarkable man should be a confectioner and pastry-cook, and this anomaly quite disturbed Penny's dreams. Her brothers, she knew, laughed at men who couldn't sit on horseback well, and called them tailors; but her brothers were very rough, and were quite without that power of anecdote which made Mr Freely such a delightful companion. He was a very good man, she thought, for she had heard him say at Mr Luff's, one day, that he always wished to do his duty in whatever state of life he might be placed; and he knew a great deal of poetry, for one day he had repeated a verse of a song. She wondered if he had made the words of the valentine!—it ended in this way:—

> 'Without thee, it is pain to live,
> But with thee, it were sweet to die'.*

Poor Mr Freely! her father would very likely object—she felt sure he would, for he always called Mr Freely 'that sugar-plum fellow'. Oh, it was very cruel, when true love was crossed in that way, and all because Mr Freely was a confectioner: well, Penny would be true to him, for all that, and since his being a confectioner gave her an opportunity of showing her faithfulness, she was glad of it. Edward Freely was a pretty name, much better than John Towers. Young Towers had offered her a rose out of his button-hole the other day, blushing very much; but she refused it, and thought with delight how much Mr Freely would be comforted if he knew her firmness of mind.

Poor little Penny! the days were so very long among the daisies on a grazing farm, and thought is so active—how was it possible that the inward drama should not get the start of the outward? I have known young ladies, much better educated, and with an outward world diversified by instructive lectures, to say nothing of literature and highly-developed fancy-work, who have spun a cocoon of visionary joys and sorrows for themselves, just as Penny did. Her elder sister, Letitia, who had a prouder style of beauty, and a more worldly ambition, was engaged to a wool-factor, who came all the way from Cattelton to see her; and everybody knows that a wool-factor takes a very high rank, sometimes driving a double-bodied gig. Letty's notions got higher every day, and Penny never dared to speak of her cherished griefs to her lofty sister—never dared to propose that they should call at Mr Freely's to buy liquorice, though she had prepared for such an incident by mentioning a slight sore throat. So she had to pass the shop on the other side of the market-place, and reflect, with a suppressed sigh, that behind those pink and white jars somebody was thinking of her tenderly, unconscious of the small space that divided her from him.

And it was quite true that, when business permitted, Mr Freely thought a great deal of Penny. He thought her prettiness comparable to the loveliest things in confectionery; he judged her to be of sub-missive temper—likely to wait upon him as well as if she had been a negress, and to be silently terrified when his liver made him irritable; and he considered the Palfrey family quite the best in the parish, possessing marriageable daughters. On the whole, he thought her worthy to become Mrs Edward Freely, and all the more so, because it would probably require some ingenuity to win her. Mr Palfrey was capable of horse-whipping a too rash pretender to his daughter's hand; and, moreover, he had three tall sons: it was clear that a suitor would be at a disadvantage with such a family, unless travel and natural acumen had given him a countervailing power of contriv-ance. And the first idea that occurred to him in the matter was, that

Mr Palfrey would object less if he knew that the Freelys were a much higher family than his own. It had been foolish modesty in him hitherto to conceal the fact that a branch of the Freelys held a manor in Yorkshire, and to shut up the portrait of his great uncle the admiral, instead of hanging it up where a family portrait should be hung—over the mantelpiece in the parlour. Admiral Freely, K.C.B.,* once placed in this conspicuous position, was seen to have had one arm only, and one eye,—in these points resembling the heroic Nelson*,—while a certain pallid insignificance of feature confirmed the relationship between himself and his grand-nephew.

Next, Mr Freely was seized with an irrepressible ambition to possess Mrs Palfrey's receipt for brawn, hers being pronounced on all hands to be superior to his own—as he informed her in a very flattering letter carried by his errand-boy. Now Mrs Palfrey, like other geniuses, wrought by instinct rather than by rule, and possessed no receipts,—indeed, despised all people who used them, observing that people who pickled by book, must pickle by weights and measures, and such nonsense; as for herself, her weights and measures were the tip of her finger and the tip of her tongue, and if you went nearer, why, of course, for dry goods like flour and spice, you went by handfuls and pinches, and for wet, there was a middle-sized jug—quite the best thing whether for much or little, because you might know how much a teacupful was if you'd got any use of your senses, and you might be sure it would take five middle-sized jugs to make a gallon. Knowledge of this kind is like Titian's* colouring, difficult to communicate; and as Mrs Palfrey, once remarkably handsome, had now become rather stout and asthmatical, and scarcely ever left home, her oral teaching could hardly be given anywhere except at Long Meadows. Even a matron is not insusceptible to flattery, and the prospect of a visitor whose great object would be to listen to her conversation, was not without its charms to Mrs Palfrey. Since there was no receipt to be sent in reply to Mr Freely's humble request, she called on her more docile daughter, Penny, to write a note, telling him that her mother would be glad to see him and talk with him on brawn, any day that he could call at Long Meadows. Penny obeyed with a trembling hand, thinking how wonderfully things came about in this world.

In this way, Mr Freely got himself introduced into the home of the Palfreys, and notwithstanding a tendency in the male part of the family to jeer at him a little as 'peaky' and bow-legged, he presently established his position as an accepted and frequent guest. Young Towers looked at him with increasing disgust when they met at the house on a Sunday, and secretly longed to try his ferret upon him, as a piece of vermin which that valuable animal would be likely to tackle with unhesitating vigour. But—so blind sometimes are parents—neither Mr nor Mrs Palfrey suspected that Penny would have anything to say to a tradesman of questionable rank whose youthful bloom was much withered. Young Towers, they thought, had an eye to her, and *that* was likely enough to be a match some day; but Penny was a child at present. And all the while Penny was imagining the circumstances under which Mr Freely would make her an offer: perhaps down by the row of damson-trees, when they were in the garden before tea; perhaps by letter—in which case, how would the letter begin? 'Dearest Penelope?' or 'My dear Miss Penelope?' or straight off, without dear anything, as seemed the most natural when people were embarrassed? But, however he might make the offer, she would not accept it without her father's consent: she would always be true to Mr Freely, but she would not disobey her father. For Penny was a good girl, though some of her female friends were afterwards of opinion that it spoke ill for her not to have felt an instinctive repugnance to Mr Freely.

But he was cautious, and wished to be quite sure of the ground he trod on. His views in marriage were not entirely sentimental, but were as duly mingled with considerations of what would be advantageous to a man in his position, as if he had had a very large amount of money spent on his education. He was not a man to fall in love in the wrong place; and so, he applied himself quite as much to conciliate the favour of the parents, as to secure the attachment of Penny. Mrs Palfrey had not been inaccessible to flattery, and her husband, being also of mortal mould, would not, it might be hoped, be proof against rum—that very fine Jamaica rum of which Mr Freely expected always to have a supply sent him from Jamaica. It was not easy to get Mr Palfrey into the parlour behind the shop, where a mild back-street light fell on the features of the heroic admiral; but by getting hold of him rather late one evening as he was about to return home from Grimworth, the aspiring lover succeeded in persuading him to sup on some collared beef which, after Mrs Palfrey's brawn, he would find the very best of cold eating.

From that hour Mr Freely felt sure of success: being in privacy with an estimable man old enough to be his father, and being rather lonely in the world, it was natural he should unbosom himself a little on subjects which he could not speak of in a mixed circle—especially concerning his expectations from his uncle in Jamaica, who had no children, and loved his nephew Edward better than any one else in the world, though he had been so hurt at his leaving Jamaica, that he had threatened to cut him off with a shilling. However, he had since written to state his full forgiveness, and though he was an eccentric old gentleman and could not bear to give away money during his life, Mr Edward Freely could show Mr Palfrey the letter which declared, plainly enough, who would be the affectionate uncle's heir. Mr Palfrey actually saw the letter, and could not help admiring the spirit of the nephew who declared that such brilliant hopes as these made no difference to his conduct; he should work at his humble business and make his modest fortune at it all the same. If the Jamaica estate was to come to him—well and good. It was nothing very surprising for one of the Freely family to have an estate left him, considering the lands that family had possessed in time gone by,—nay, still possessed in the Northumberland branch. Would not Mr Palfrey take another glass of rum? and also look at the last year's balance of the accounts? Mr Freely was a man who cared to possess personal virtues, and did not pique himself on his family, though some men would.

We know how easily the great Leviathan* may be led, when once there is a hook in his nose or a bridle in his jaws. Mr Palfrey was a large man, but, like Leviathan's, his bulk went against him when once he had taken a turning. He was not a mercurial man, who easily changed his point of view. Enough. Before two months were over, he had given his consent to Mr Freely's marriage with his daughter Penny, and having hit on a formula by which he could justify it, fenced off all doubts and objections, his own included. The formula was this: 'I'm not a man to put my nose up an entry before I know where it leads.'

Little Penny was very proud and fluttering—but hardly so happy as she expected to be in an engagement. She wondered if young Towers cared much about it, for he had not been to the house lately, and her sister and brothers were rather inclined to sneer than to sympathize. Grimworth rang with the news. All men extolled Mr Freely's good fortune; while the women, with the tender solicitude characteristic of the sex, wished the marriage might turn out well.

While affairs were at this triumphant juncture, Mr Freely one morning observed that a stone-carver who had been breakfasting in the eating-room had left a newspaper behind. It was the 'X-shire Gazette', and X-shire being a county not unknown to Mr Freely, he felt some curiosity to glance over it, and especially over the advertisements. A slight flush came over his face as he read. It was produced by the following announcement:—'If David Faux, son of Jonathan Faux, late of Gilsbrook, will apply at the office of Mr Strutt, attorney, of Rodham, he will hear of something to his advantage.'

'Father's dead!' exclaimed Mr Freely, involuntarily. 'Can he have left me a legacy?'

CHAPTER III

PERHAPS it was a result quite different from your expectations, that Mr David Faux should have returned from the West Indies only a few years after his arrival there, and have set up in his old business, like any plain man who had never travelled. But these cases do occur in life. Since, as we know, men change their skies and see new constellations without changing their souls, it will follow sometimes that they don't change their business under those novel circumstances.

Certainly, this result was contrary to David's own expectations. He had looked forward, you are aware, to a brilliant career among 'the blacks'; but, either because they had already seen too many white men, or for some other reason, they did not at once recognize him as a superior order of human being; besides, there were no princesses among them. Nobody in Jamaica was anxious to maintain David for the mere pleasure of his society; and those hidden merits of a man which are so well known to himself were as little recognized there as they notoriously are in the effete society of the Old World. So that in the dark hints that David threw out at the Oyster Club about that life of Sultanic self-indulgence spent by him in the luxurious Indies, I really think he was doing himself a wrong; I believe he worked for his bread, and, in fact, took to cooking again, as, after all, the only department in which he could offer skilled labour. He had formed several ingenious plans by which he meant to circumvent people of large fortune and small faculty; but then he never met with exactly the right people under exactly the right circumstances. David's devices for getting rich without work had apparently no direct relation with the world outside him, as his confectionery receipts had. It is possible to pass a great many bad halfpennies and bad half-crowns, but I believe there has no instance been known of passing a halfpenny or a half-crown as a sovereign. A sharper can drive a brisk trade in this world: it is undeniable that there may be a fine career for him, if he will dare consequences; but David was too timid to be a sharper, or venture in any way among the man-traps of the law. He dared rob nobody but his mother. And so he had to fall back on the genuine value there was in him—to be content to pass as a good halfpenny, or, to speak more accurately, as a good confectioner. For in spite of some additional reading and observation, there was nothing else he could make so much money by; nay, he found in himself even a capability of extending his skill in this direction, and embracing all forms of cookery; while, in other branches of human labour, he began to see that it was not possible for him to shine. Fate was too strong for him; he had thought to master her inclination and had fled over the seas to that end; but she caught him, tied an apron round him, and snatching him from all other devices, made him devise cakes and patties in a kitchen at Kingstown. He was getting submissive to her, since she paid him with tolerable gains; but fevers and prickly heat, and other evils incidental to cooks in ardent climates, made him long for his native land; so he took ship once more, carrying his six years' savings, and seeing distinctly, this time, what were Fate's intentions as to his career. If you question me closely as to whether all the money with which he set up at Grimworth consisted of pure and simple earnings, I am obliged to confess that he got a sum or two for charitably abstaining from mentioning some other people's misdemeanours. Altogether, since no prospects were attached to his family name, and since a new christening seemed a suitable commencement of a new life, Mr David Faux thought it as well to call himself Mr Edward Freely.

But lo! now, in opposition to all calculable probability, some benefit appeared to be attached to the name of David Faux. Should he neglect it, as beneath the attention of a prosperous tradesman? It might bring him into contact with his family again, and he felt no yearnings in that direction: moreover, he had small belief that the 'something to his advantage' could be anything considerable. On the other hand, even a small gain is pleasant, and the promise of it in this instance was so surprising, that David felt his curiosity awakened. The scale dipped at last on the side of writing to the lawyer, and, to be brief, the correspondence ended in an appointment for a meeting between David and his eldest brother at Mr Strutt's, the vague 'something' having been defined as a legacy from his father of eighty-two pounds three shillings.

David, you know, had expected to be disinherited; and so he would have been, if he had not, like some other indifferent sons, come of excellent parents, whose conscience made them scrupulous where much more highly-instructed people often feel themselves warranted in following the bent of their indignation. Good Mrs

Faux could never forget that she had brought this ill-conditioned son into the world when he was in that entirely helpless state which excluded the smallest choice on his part; and, somehow or other, she felt that his going wrong would be his father's and mother's fault, if they failed in one tittle of their parental duty. Her notion of parental duty was not of a high and subtle kind, but it included giving him his due share of the family property; for when a man had got a little honest money of his own, was he so likely to steal? To cut the delinquent son off with a shilling, was like delivering him over to his evil propensities. No; let the sum of twenty guineas which he had stolen be deducted from his share, and then let the sum of three guineas be put back from it, seeing that his mother had always considered three of the twenty guineas as his; and, though he had run away, and was, perhaps, gone across the sea, let the money be left to him all the same, and be kept in reserve for his possible return. Mr Faux agreed to his wife's views, and made a codicil to his will accordingly, in time to die with a clear conscience. But for some time his family thought it likely that David would never reappear; and the eldest son, who had the charge of Jacob on his hands, often thought it a little hard that David might perhaps be dead, and yet, for want of certitude on that point, his legacy could not fall to his legal heir. But in this state of things the opposite certitude—namely, that David was still alive and in England—seemed to be brought by the testimony of a neighbour, who, having been on a journey to Cattelton, was pretty sure he had seen David in a gig, with a stout man driving by his side. He could 'swear it was David', though he could 'give no account why, for he had no marks on him; but no more had a white dog, and that didn't hinder folks from knowing a white dog.' It was this incident which had led to the advertisement.

The legacy was paid, of course, after a few preliminary disclosures as to Mr David's actual position. He begged to send his love to his mother, and to say that he hoped to pay her a dutiful visit by-and-by; but, at present, his business and near prospect of marriage made it difficult for him to leave home. His brother replied with much frankness.

'My mother may do as she likes about having you to see her, but, for my part, I don't want to catch sight of you on the premises again. When folks have taken a new name, they'd better keep to their new 'quinetance.'

David pocketed the insult along with the eighty-two pounds three, and travelled home again in some triumph at the ease of a transaction which had enriched him to this extent. He had no intention of offending his brother by further claims on his fraternal recognition, and relapsed with full contentment into the character of Mr Edward Freely, the orphan, scion of a great but reduced family, with an eccentric uncle in the West Indies. (I have already hinted that he had some acquaintance with imaginative literature; and being of a practical turn, he had, you perceive, applied even this form of knowledge to practical purposes.)

It was little more than a week after the return from his fruitful journey, that the day of his marriage with Penny having been fixed, it was agreed that Mrs Palfrey should overcome her reluctance to move from home, and that she and her husband should bring their two daughters to inspect little Penny's future abode and decide on the new arrangements to be made for the reception of the bride. Mr Freely meant her to have a house so pretty and comfortable that she need not envy even a wool-factor's wife. Of course, the upper room over the shop was to be the best sitting-room; but also the parlour behind the shop was to be made a suitable bower for the lovely Penny, who would naturally wish to be near her husband, though Mr Freely declared his resolution never to allow *his* wife to wait in the shop. The decisions about the parlour furniture were left till last, because the party was to take tea there; and, about five o'clock, they were all seated there with the best muffins and buttered buns before them, little Penny blushing and smiling, with her 'crop' in the best order, and a blue frock showing her little white shoulders, while her opinion was being always asked and never given. She secretly wished to have a particular sort of chimney ornaments, but she could not have brought herself to mention it. Seated by the side of her yellow and rather withered lover, who, though he had not reached his thirtieth year, had already crow's-feet about his eyes, she was quite tremulous at the greatness of her lot in being married to a man who had travelled so much—and before her sister Letty! The handsome Letitia looked rather proud and contemptuous, thought her future brother-in-law an odious person, and was vexed with her father and mother for letting Penny marry him. Dear little Penny! She certainly did look like a fresh white-heart cherry going to be bitten off the stem by that lipless mouth.

Would no deliverer come to make a slip between that cherry and that mouth without a lip?*

'Quite a family likeness between the admiral and you, Mr Freely,' observed Mrs Palfrey, who was looking at the family portrait for the first time. 'It's wonderful! and only a grand-uncle. Do you feature the rest of your family, as you know of?'

'I can't say,' said Mr Freely, with a sigh. 'My family have mostly thought themselves too high to take any notice of me.'

At this moment an extraordinary disturbance was heard in the shop, as of a heavy animal stamping about and making angry noises, and then of a glass vessel falling in shivers, while the voice of the apprentice was heard calling 'Master' in great alarm.

Mr Freely rose in anxious astonishment, and hastened into the shop, followed by the four Palfreys, who made a group at the parlour-door, transfixed with wonder at seeing a large man in a smock-frock, with a pitchfork in his hand, rush up to Mr Freely and hug him, crying out,—'Zavy, Zavy, b'other Zavy!'

It was Jacob, and for some moments David lost all presence of mind. He felt arrested for having stolen his mother's guineas. He turned cold, and trembled in his brother's grasp.

'Why, how's this?' said Mr Palfrey, advancing from the door. 'Who is he?'

Jacob supplied the answer by saying over and over again,—

'I'se Zacob, b'other Zacob. Come 'o zee Zavy'—till hunger prompted him to relax his grasp, and to seize a large raised pie, which he lifted to his mouth.

By this time David's power of device had begun to return, but it was a very hard task for his prudence to master his rage and hatred towards poor Jacob.

'I don't know who he is; he must be drunk,' he said, in a low tone to Mr Palfrey. 'But he's dangerous with that pitchfork. He'll never let it go.' Then checking himself on the point of betraying too great an intimacy with Jacob's habits, he added: '*You* watch him, while I run for the constable.' And he hurried out of the shop.

'Why, where do you come from, my man?' said Mr Palfrey, speaking to Jacob in a conciliatory tone. Jacob was eating pie by large mouthfuls, and looking round at the other good things in the shop, while he embraced his pitchfork with his left arm and laid his left hand on some Bath buns. He was in the rare position of a person who recovers a long absent friend and finds him richer than ever in the characteristics that won his heart.

'I's Zacob—b'other Zacob—'t home. I love Zavy—b'other Zavy,' he said, as soon as Mr Palfrey had drawn his attention. 'Zavy come back from z' Indies—got mother's zinnies. Where's Zavy?' he added, looking round and then turning to the others with a question-ing air, puzzled by David's disappearance.

'It's very odd,' observed Mr Palfrey to his wife and daughters. 'He seems to say Freely's his brother come back from th' Indies.'

'What a pleasant relation for us!' said Letitia sarcastically. 'I think he's a good deal like Mr Freely. He's got just the same sort of nose, and his eyes are the same colour.'

Poor Penny was ready to cry.

But now Mr Freely re-entered the shop without the constable. During his walk of a few yards he had had time and calmness enough to widen his view of consequences, and he saw that to get Jacob taken to the workhouse or to the lock-up house as an offensive stranger, might have awkward effects if his family took the trouble of inquiring after him. He must resign himself to more patient measures.

'On second thoughts,' he said, beckoning to Mr Palfrey and whispering to him while Jacob's back was turned, 'he's a poor half-witted fellow. Perhaps his friends will come after him. I don't mind giving him something to eat, and letting him lie down for the night. He's got it into his head that he knows me—they do get these fan-cies, idiots do. He'll perhaps go away again in an hour or two, and make no more ado. I'm a kind-hearted man *myself*—I shouldn't like to have the poor fellow ill-used.'

'Why, he'll eat a sovereign's worth in no time,' said Mr Palfrey, thinking Mr Freely a little too magnificent in his generosity.

'Eh, Zavy, come back?' exclaimed Jacob, giving his dear brother another hug, which crushed Mr Freely's features inconveniently against the stale of the pitchfork.

'Ay, ay,' said Mr Freely, smiling, with every capability of murder in his mind, except the courage to commit it. He wished the Bath buns might by chance have arsenic in them.

'Mother's zinnies?' said Jacob, pointing to a glass jar of yellow lozenges that stood in the window. 'Zive 'em me.'

David dared not do otherwise than reach down the glass jar and give Jacob a handful. He received them in his smock-frock, which he held out for more.

'They'll keep him quiet a bit, at any rate,' thought David, and emptied the jar. Jacob grinned and mowed with delight.

'You're very good to this stranger, Mr Freely,' said Letitia; and then spitefully, as David joined the party at the parlour-door, 'I think you could hardly treat him better, if he was really your brother.'

'I've always thought it a duty to be good to idiots,' said Mr Freely, striving after the most moral view of the subject. 'We might have been idiots ourselves—everybody might have been born idiots, instead of having their right senses.'

'I don't know where there'd ha' been victual for us all then,' observed Mrs Palfrey, regarding the matter in a housewifely light.

'But let us sit down again and finish our tea,' said Mr Freely. 'Let us leave the poor creature to himself.'

They walked into the parlour again; but Jacob, not, apparently, appreciating the kindness of leaving him to himself, immediately followed his brother, and seated himself, pitchfork grounded, at the table.

'Well,' said Miss Letitia, rising, 'I don't know whether *you* mean to stay, mother; but I shall go home.'

'Oh, me too,' said Penny, frightened to death at Jacob, who had begun to nod and grin at her.

'Well, I think we *had* better be going, Mr Palfrey,' said the mother, rising more slowly.

Mr Freely, whose complexion had become decidedly yellower during the last half-hour, did not resist this proposition. He hoped they should meet again 'under happier circumstances'.

'It's my belief the man is his brother,' said Letitia, when they were all on their way home.

'Letty, it's very ill-natured of you,' said Penny, beginning to cry.

'Nonsense!' said Mr Palfrey. 'Freely's got no brother—he's said so many and many a time; he's an orphan; he's got nothing but uncles—leastwise, one. What's it matter what an idiot says? What call had Freely to tell lies?'

Letitia tossed her head and was silent.

Mr Freely, left alone with his affectionate brother Jacob, brooded over the possibility of luring him out of the town early the next morning, and getting him conveyed to Gilsbrook without further betrayals. But the thing was difficult. He saw clearly that if he took Jacob away himself, his absence, conjoined with the disappearance of the stranger, would either cause the conviction that he was really a relative, or would oblige him to the dangerous course of inventing a story to account for his disappearance, and his own absence at the same time. David groaned. There come occasions when falsehood is felt to be inconvenient. It would, perhaps, have been a longer-headed device, if he had never told any of those clever fibs about his uncles, grand and otherwise; for the Palfreys were simple people, and shared the popular prejudice against lying. Even if he could get Jacob away this time, what security was there that he would not come again, having once found the way? O guineas! O lozenges! what enviable people those were who had never robbed their mothers, and had never told fibs! David spent a sleepless night, while Jacob was snoring close by. Was this the upshot of travelling to the Indies, and acquiring experience combined with anecdote?

He rose at break of day, as he had once before done when he was in fear of Jacob, and took all gentle means to rouse him from his deep sleep; he dared not be loud, because his apprentice was in the house, and would report everything. But Jacob was not to be roused. He fought out with his fist at the unknown cause of disturbance, turned over, and snored again. He must be left to wake as he would. David, with a cold perspiration on his brow, confessed to himself that Jacob could not be got away that day.

Mr Palfrey came over to Grimworth before noon, with a natural curiosity to see how his future son-in-law got on with the stranger to whom he was so benevolently inclined. He found a crowd round the shop. All Grimworth by this time had heard how Freely had been fastened on by an idiot, who called him 'Brother Zavy'; and the younger population seemed to find the singular stranger an unwearying source of fascination, while the householders dropped in one by one to inquire into the incident.

'Why don't you send him to the workhouse?' said Mr Prettyman. 'You'll have a row with him and the children presently, and he'll eat you up. The workhouse is the proper place for him; let his kin claim him, if he's got any.'

'Those may be *your* feelings, Mr Prettyman,' said David, his mind quite enfeebled by the torture of his position.

'What, *is* he your brother, then?' said Mr Prettyman, looking at his neighbour Freely rather sharply.

'All men are our brothers, and idiots particular so,' said Mr Freely, who, like many other men of extensive knowledge, was not master of the English language.

'Come, come, if he's your brother, tell the truth, man,' said Mr Prettyman, with growing suspicion. 'Don't be ashamed of your own flesh and blood.'

Mr Palfrey was present, and also had his eye on Freely. It is difficult for a man to believe in the advantage of a truth which will disclose him to have been a liar. In this critical moment, David shrank from this immediate disgrace in the eyes of his future father-in-law.

'Mr Prettyman,' he said, 'I take your observations as an insult. I've no reason to be otherwise than proud of my own flesh and blood. If this poor man was my brother more than all men are, I should say so.'

A tall figure darkened the door, and David, lifting his eyes in that direction, saw his eldest brother, Jonathan, on the door-sill.

'I'll stay wi' Zavy,' shouted Jacob, as he, too, caught sight of his eldest brother; and, running behind the counter, he clutched David hard.

'What, he *is* here?' said Jonathan Faux, coming forward. 'My mother would have no nay, as he'd been away so long, but I must see after him. And it struck me he was very like come after you, because we'd been talking of you o' late, and where you lived.'

David saw there was no escape; he smiled a ghastly smile.

'What, is this a relation of yours, sir?' said Mr Palfrey to Jonathan.

'Ay, it's my innicent of a brother, sure enough,' said honest Jonathan. 'A fine trouble and cost he is to us, in th' eating and other things, but we must bear what's laid on us.'

'And your name's Freely, is it?' said Mr Prettyman.

'Nay, nay, my name's Faux, I know nothing o' Freelys,' said Jonathan, curtly. 'Come,' he added, turning to David, 'I must take some news to mother about Jacob. Shall I take him with me, or will you undertake to send him back?'

'Take him, if you can make him loose his hold of me,' said David, feebly.

'Is this gentleman here in the confectionery line your brother, then sir?' said Mr Prettyman, feeling that it was an occasion on which formal language must be used.

'*I* don't want to own him,' said Jonathan, unable to resist a movement of indignation that had never been allowed to satisfy itself. 'He run away from home with good reasons in his pocket years ago: he didn't want to be owned again, I reckon.'

Mr Palfrey left the shop; he felt his own pride too severely wounded by the sense that he had let himself be fooled, to feel curiosity for further details. The most pressing business was to go home and tell his daughter that Freely was a poor sneak, probably a rascal, and that her engagement was broken off.

Mr Prettyman stayed, with some internal self-gratulation that *he* had never given in to Freely, and that Mr Chaloner would see now what sort of fellow it was that he had put over the heads of older parishioners. He considered it due from him (Mr Prettyman) that, for the interests of the parish, he should know all that was to be known about this 'interloper'. Grimworth would have people coming from Botany Bay to settle in it, if things went on in this way.

It soon appeared that Jacob could not be made to quit his dear brother David except by force. He understood, with a clearness equal to that of the most intelligent mind, that Jonathan would take him back to skimmed milk, apple-dumpling, broad-beans, and pork. And he had found a paradise in his brother's shop. It was a difficult matter to use force with Jacob, for he wore heavy nailed boots; and if his pitchfork had been mastered, he would have resorted without hesitation to kicks. Nothing short of using guile to bind him hand and foot would have made all parties safe.

'Let him stay,' said David, with desperate resignation, frightened above all things at the idea of further disturbances in his shop, which would make his exposure all the more conspicuous. '*You* go away again, and to-morrow I can, perhaps, get him to go to Gilsbrook with me. He'll follow me fast enough, I daresay,' he added, with a half groan.

'Very well,' said Jonathan, gruffly. 'I don't see why *you* shouldn't have some trouble and expense with him as well as the rest of us. But mind you bring him back safe and soon, else mother'll never rest.'

On this arrangement being concluded, Mr Prettyman begged Mr Jonathan Faux to go and take a snack with him, an invitation which was quite acceptable; and as honest Jonathan had nothing to be ashamed of, it is probable that he was very frank in his communications to the civil draper, who, pursuing the benefit of the parish, hastened to make all the information he could gather about Freely common parochial property. You may imagine that the meeting of the Club at the Woolpack that evening was unusually lively. Every member was anxious to prove that he had never liked Freely, as he called himself. Faux was his name, was it? Fox would have been more suitable. The majority expressed a desire to see him hooted out of the town.

Mr Freely did not venture over his door-sill that day, for he knew Jacob would keep at his side, and there was every probability that they would have a train of juvenile followers. He sent to engage the Woolpack gig for an early hour the next morning; but this order was not kept religiously a secret by the landlord. Mr Freely was informed that he could not have the gig till seven; and the Grimworth people were early risers. Perhaps they were more alert than usual on this particular morning; for when Jacob, with a bag of sweets in his hand, was induced to mount the gig with his brother David, the inhabitants of the market-place were looking out of their doors and windows, and at the turning of the street there was even a muster of apprentices and schoolboys, who shouted as they passed in what Jacob took to be a very merry and friendly way, nodding and grinning in return. 'Huzzay, David Faux! how's your uncle?' was their morning's greeting. Like other pointed things, it was not altogether impromptu.

Even this public derision was not so crushing to David as the horrible thought that though he might succeed now in getting Jacob home again there would never be any security against his coming back, like a wasp to the honey-pot. As long as David lived at Grimworth, Jacob's return would be hanging over him. But could he go on living at Grimworth—an object of ridicule, discarded by the Palfreys, after having revelled in the consciousness that he was an envied and prosperous confectioner? David liked to be envied; he minded less about being loved.

His doubts on this point were soon settled. The mind of Grimworth became obstinately set against him and his viands, and the new school being finished, the eating-room was closed. If there had been no other reason, sympathy with the Palfreys, that respectable family who had lived in the parish time out of mind, would have determined all well-to-do people to decline Freely's goods. Besides, he had absconded with his mother's guineas: who knew what else he had done, in Jamaica or elsewhere, before he came to Grimworth, worming himself into families under false pretences? Females shuddered. Dreadful suspicions gathered round him: his green eyes, his bow-legs, had a criminal aspect. The rector disliked the sight of a man who had imposed upon him; and all boys who could not afford to purchase, hooted 'David Faux' as they passed his shop. Certainly no man now would pay anything for the 'goodwill' of Mr Freely's business, and he would be obliged to quit it without a peculium* so desirable towards defraying the expense of moving.

In a few months the shop in the market-place was again to let, and Mr David Faux, *alias* Mr Edward Freely, had gone—nobody at Grimworth knew whither. In this way the demoralization of Grimworth women was checked. Young Mrs Steene renewed her efforts to make light mince-pies, and having at last made a batch so excellent that Mr Steene looked at her with complacency as he ate them, and said they were the best he had ever eaten in his life, she thought less of bulbuls and renegades ever after. The secrets of the finer cookery were revived in the breasts of matronly housewives, and daughters were again anxious to be initiated in them.

You will further, I hope, be glad to hear, that some purchases of drapery made by pretty Penny, in preparation for her marriage with Mr Freely, came in quite as well for her wedding with young Towers as if they had been made expressly for the latter occasion. For Penny's complexion had not altered, and blue always became it best.

Here ends the story of Mr David Faux, confectioner, and his brother Jacob. And we see in it, I think, an admirable instance of the unexpected forms in which the great Nemesis hides herself.

EXPLANATORY NOTES

I AM indebted to earlier editions and critical discussions of 'The Lifted Veil' and 'Brother Jacob', in particular Beryl Gray's Afterwords to her Virago editions of 1985 and 1989, and Peter Mudford's Everyman edition of 1996. I am particularly grateful to Margaret Harris and Judith Johnston for permitting me to see a proof copy of *The Journals of George Eliot* (Cambridge, 1998). For references to Geneva, Prague, and Vienna, I have drawn particularly on John Murray's popular handbooks for English travellers on the Continent.

THE LIFTED VEIL

1 *Title*: probably an allusion to Shelley's sonnet of 1824:

> Lift not the painted veil which those who live
> Call Life . . .

There may also be an echo of William Collins's 'Ode to Fear' (1746):

> Thou, to whom the world unknown
> With all its shadowy shapes is shown;
> Who see'st appalled the unreal scene,
> While Fancy lifts the veil between:
> Ah Fear! Ah frantic Fear!

Truth has from ancient times been represented as a veiled place or figure. In Plutarch's *Moralia* (354c) the inscription upon the temple of Isis at Sais reads: 'I am everything that has been, that is, and that ever shall be: no human mortal has discovered me behind my veil'. Relatedly, death has often been described as a place or state 'behind' or 'beyond' the veil— Tennyson's *In Memoriam* asks: 'What hope of answer, or redress? | Behind the veil, behind the veil' (lvi. 27–8). 'The Lifted Veil' thus suggests knowledge both of ultimate truths and of death. For its mesmeric resonances see Malcolm Bull, 'Mastery and Slavery in *The Lifted Veil*', *Essays in Criticism*, 48 (1998), discussed in Introduction, p. xx.

2 *Epigraph*: not present on first publication. George Eliot composed the motto in February 1873 to express 'the idea which [the story] embodies and which justifies its painfulness'. At that date she did not think it 'judicious' to reprint 'The Lifted Veil'. When it was, eventually, reissued in the Cabinet Edition of 1878 the motto became the story's epigraph.

3 *angina pectoris*: according to the *Encyclopaedia Britannica* (8th edn., 1853) a term used by physicians 'to signify an anomalous or spasmodic affection of the chest, commonly connected with a diseased state of the heart or great bloodvessels'. In this period, however, the terminology was shifting slightly, and angina was beginning to be understood as 'a *neurosis*

<u>or nervous affection of the heart</u>' (*Encyclopaedia Britannica*, 1875). Eliot repeatedly made disease of the heart an affliction of her less sympathetic male characters: in addition to Latimer one thinks of the selfish young Captain Wybrow (attended by Dr Hart) in 'Mr Gilfil's Love-Story' (*Scenes of Clerical Life*), and Mr Casaubon in *Middlemarch*.

4 *ubi sæva indignatio ulterius cor lacerare nequit*: 'where savage indignation can no longer lacerate the heart'.

6 *those dead but sceptred spirits*: a misquotation of Byron's *Manfred* (1817), III. iv. 38–41:

> The heart ran o'er
> With silent worship of the great of old!—
> The dead, but sceptred, sovereigns, who still rule
> Our spirits from their urns—

Potter's 'Æschylus' . . . Francis's 'Horace': Robert Potter's *The Tragedies of Æschylus* (1777) and the Revd Philip Francis's *Poetical Translation of the Works of Horace* (1747) were standard English annotated verse translations.

mining speculations: a reference to the Government School of Mines, established in Jermyn St, London, in 1851, extending the work of the Museum of Economic Geology which, since 1841, had been offering instruction in analytical chemistry, metallurgy, and mineralogy. There had long been pressure from various quarters—notably the British Association for the Advancement of Science (founded 1831)—to reform school curricula, placing far more emphasis on the sciences and less on classics and religion. The evolutionist T. H. Huxley, who lectured at the School of Mines, was among the most prominent of those campaigning to 'break the Latin stranglehold, so that a schoolboy would in future know "the difference between . . . the contents of his skull and those of his abdomen"'. The cause was advanced by the establishment in 1853 of a Government Department of Science and Art (i.e. Technology), and by the appointment of the chemist Lyon Playfair as Secretary for Science. (See Adrian Desmond, *Huxley: The Devil's Disciple* (London, 1994), 189–90, and, on the related pressure for the secularization of education, [George Combe], 'Secular Education', *The Westminster Review*, 58 (July 1852), 1–32.) The Government School of Mines became, in 1863, the Royal School of Mines and of Science Applied to the Arts, and eventually evolved into today's Imperial College.

Mr Letherall: Mr Letherall is a phrenologist, and claims to be able to analyse people's intellectual, emotional, and moral faculties from the bumps of their skulls. According to George Combe's *Elements of Phrenology* (1824), the leading book on the subject, a deficiency in the area along the eyebrows indicates a lack of order or method in the arranging of objects and, more generally, in the faculty for systematizing, classifying, and generalizing; also weak powers of judging time and of

calculating (Latimer's nervousness about meeting his father's expectation of punctuality is noted on p. 11). An excess at the upper sides of the
head suggests an abnormal capacity for wonder and 'ideality'—'a manner
of feeling and of thinking, befitting the regions of fancy more than the
abodes of men' and 'essential to the poet, painter, sculptor, and all who
cultivate the fine arts' (Combe, *Elements*, 69). Mr Letherall's insistence on
a corrective education accords with the Combean emphasis on the adaptive powers of the mind. George Eliot had a long-standing interest in
phrenology. She had read the *Elements of Phrenology* and in July 1844 had
had a cast of her head made by James Deville of the Strand for her friend
Charles Bray, a passionate advocate of phrenology. When shown the cast
Combe took it to be that of a man. He analysed her head in person in
August 1851, declaring her 'the ablest woman whom I have seen', with 'a
very large brain', 'great analytic power and an instinctive soundness of
judgment'. She corresponded with Combe in early 1852 after he wrote to
her complaining about the *Westminster Review*'s perceived unwillingness to
admit discussion of either phrenology or mesmerism. (See B. M. Gray,
'Pseudoscience and George Eliot's "The Lifted Veil" ', *Nineteenth-Century
Fiction*, 36/4 (1982), 407–23, and Rosemary Ashton, *George Eliot: A Life*
(London, 1996), 3, 89, 54.) Charles Bray accused her more directly in
1855 of having lost faith in the 'physiological basis' of phrenology—by
implication under G. H. Lewes's influence (see *Letters*, ii. 210). Lewes was
certainly sceptical of the field's scientific claims, and put his views in print
in the revised edition of the *Biographical Dictionary of Philosophy* (1857).
He was duly attacked in Bray's *Philosophy of Necessity* (2nd edn., 1863,
144–9).

6 *academy*: at this point the following lines were deleted from the *Blackwood's* text: ';whence I have been led to conclude that the only universal
rule with regard to education is, that no rule should be held to be universal, a good education being that which adapts itself to individual wants
and faculties'.

Plutarch: Greek prose writer (first century AD) whose popularity rests
mainly on his 46 *Parallel Lives*—biographies in parallel of famous Greeks
and Romans, comparing, for example, Theseus and Romulus as founders
of their respective states, Alexander and Caesar as builders of the Greek
and Roman empires.

7 *Geneva*: Mary Anne Evans first visited Geneva in July 1849 just after the
death of her father. She travelled with Charles and Clara Bray and was, by
her own account, a poor companion: 'peevish' and 'utterly morbid'. On
the Brays' return to England at the end of July she took lodgings in a
pension and remained in the city for the winter. The description of Geneva
in 'The Lifted Veil' draws closely on her recollections.

Jean Jacques: Rousseau (1712–78), Geneva-born novelist and political
philosopher who was a major influence on the development of Romantic
sensibilities and attitudes. Rousseau describes the experience of boating

on Lake Bienne in the 'Cinquième promenade' ('Fifth Walk') of his *Rêveries du promeneur solitaire* (1782; *Reveries of a Solitary Walker*, Penguin edn., 1979, 85) and in Book 12 of his *Confessions* (1782; Penguin edn., 1953, 594). Eliot was deeply impressed by her reading of Rousseau from 1846 onward. When she met Ralph Waldo Emerson in July 1848 she told him that the *Confessions* had been her first introduction to profound thought.

the prophet's chariot of fire: the chariot of the prophet Elijah. See 2 Kings 11.

8 *Charles Meunier*: named, according to G. S. Haight, 'for a celebrated preacher Mary Ann used to hear at Geneva'. See *George Eliot: A Biography* (Oxford, 1968), 74.

gamins: street boys, urchins.

the Salève ... Vevay: Mont Salève, an isolated mountain range in the Haute-Savoie department of south-east France, overlooking Geneva and with a fine view, from the other side, of Mont Blanc and Jura. The town of Vevey is on the far side of Lake Geneva, 11 miles from Lausanne. Eliot had visited the town in July 1849.

9 *Prague*: Eliot had visited Prague with Lewes in July 1858. He deemed it 'the most splendid city in Germany'. She, too, was strongly impressed and used it again as a setting for part of the action of *Daniel Deronda*.

the unending bridge: the imposing Carlsbrücke, or Charles Bridge, over the Moldau, connecting the Aldstadt (old town) with the Kleinseite and ornamented on each side with twenty-eight statues of saints. At the Aldstadt end of the bridge was the old watch-tower, ornamented with sculptures and arms of the countries allied with Bohemia, with its bridge-gates which protected the city from Swedish attack during the Thirty Years War. The bridge was begun under Charles IV in 1357 and completed in 1507. Eliot refers to it in her *Journal* as 'the wonderful bridge of St Jean Nepomuck with its avenue of statues'—a reference to the bronze statue of Nepomuk (8th on the right, counting from the Aldstadt) who, legend had it, was thrown into the Moldau on the order of King Wenceslaus for refusing to divulge the confessional secrets of the queen, where-upon flames burned on the water for three days over the place where he had drowned, until his body was pulled from the river. (*The Journals of George Eliot*, ed. Margaret Harris and Judith Johnston (Cambridge, 1998), hereafter cited as *J* 324.)

the palace: the Hradschin, popularly known as the Hrad. This vast palace of the Bohemian kings, with its imposing neo-classical façade, runs along the crest of the hill to the north of Prague's Kleinstadt.

10 *dissolving view*: pictures thrown on to a screen from two magic lanterns, angled so that their images overlap on a screen. By means of a pair of thin metallic shutters terminating in comb-like teeth, the picture from one could be gradually cut off at the same time as the other emerged, so

that one picture appeared to melt into the next. First demonstrated by Henry Langdon Childe in 1807, the design was improved and completed in 1818. Dissolving views became increasingly popular in the early to mid-nineteenth century with the improvements in photographic technology.

10 *Homer . . . Dante . . . Milton*: Homer's *Iliad*, Dante's *Divine Comedy*, and Milton's *Paradise Lost*. When John Fiske, disciple of Herbert Spencer and assistant librarian at Harvard, met George Eliot in 1873 he was amazed at her apparent knowledge of the whole of Homer in Greek: she 'talked of Homer as simply as she would of flat-irons' (Haight, *George Eliot*, 468). Milton she had read from an early age and his influence on her thought and prose-style has been much discussed. Dante she would study in greater depth in the winter of 1862–3 (*J* 113–15) and read again with John Cross in 1879, signing herself 'Beatrice' in a love-letter.

Novalis: the pseudonym of Friedrich Leopold von Hardenberg (1772–1801), German Romantic poet and novelist who died of pulmonary consumption.

Canaletto: Italian painter and engraver (1697–1768), famed for his paintings of the major European cities, especially his native Venice.

11 *musical box*: 'musical snuff box' in the *Blackwood's* text (Murray also noted that they were *de rigueur* with English tourists).

Water-Nixie: the water nymph or sprite of German myth and legend, usually hostile to human beings. See, for example, Goethe's ballad 'The Fisherman' (translated and discussed by Lewes in his *Life of Goethe*).

12 *German lyrics*: i.e. German Romantic lyrics of the mid-eighteenth century through to the early nineteenth. Eliot's non German-speaking readers might have known the popular selection translated into English as *Specimens of the German Lyric Poets: Consisting of Translations in Verse from the Works of Bürger, Goethe, Klopstock, Schiller, etc.* (1822).

'Monsieur ne se trouve pas bien?': 'You are unwell, Sir?'

Hôtel des Bergues: a grand establishment in the Quartier des Bergues on the left bank of the Rhône, facing the lake. The Bergues was a relatively new quarter, having sprung up since 1830 largely to service English travellers. The reading room at Monroe's bookshop on the Quai des Bergues acted as an informal information centre for English visitors. (Murray's *Handbook for Travellers in Switzerland*, 1851).

14 *portrait-painters, who are thick as weeds at Geneva*: Mary Anne Evans lodged with a portrait painter, François D'Albert Durade, between October 1849 and March 1850, when he accompanied her on the trip back to England. She sat for a portrait by him in February 1850. He made three copies of the picture, one of which he gave her. The original is now in the National Portrait Gallery, London. (He later translated several of her works into French.)

15 *affinity for*: 'sympathy with' in the *Blackwood's* text.

16 *bonne et brave femme*: good-hearted and worthy woman.

17 *opal*: traditionally associated with changeability because of the delicate play of colours (as in Shakespeare's *Twelfth Night*: 'Thy mind is a very opal'). Eliot may also have known of the old story that an opal, wrapped in a bay-leaf, could make the bearer invisible.

18 *energumen*: a person possessed by an evil spirit. Eliot may have recalled Walter Scott's *The Abbot* (1820), ch. 32, where Margaret Graeme, a fanatical Catholic who prophesies Mary Queen of Scots' escape from Lochleven, is described as 'an *Energumene*, or possessed demoniac'.

Lichtenberg Palace: a mistake for the Liechtenstein Palace in Vienna—specifically, the Picture Gallery at Prince Liechtenstein's uninhabited summer palace in the Rossau (sometimes referred to as 'the Garden Palace'), a few streets to the north-east of the Belvedere. The collection of nearly 1,500 paintings included works by Raphael, Corregio, da Vinci, and Caravaggio. Lichtenberg is a district of Berlin. George Eliot had spent the winter of 1854–5 in that city.

Giorgione's picture: described in Murray's *Handbook for Travellers* as 'Lucretia Borgia regarding a sketch of Lucretia, with an inscription'. The attribution to Giorgione was an error; after the mid-1870s the painting disappears from English guidebook recommendations but Murray's description is sufficient to identify it as a copy of Lorenzo Lotto's 'A Lady with a Drawing of Lucretia', now in the National Gallery, London. Crowe and Cavalcaselle's *History of Painting in Northern Italy* (1912) confirms this, listing the painting Eliot saw as an old copy of the Lotto, 'of feebler execution'.

19 *Belvedere Gallery*: the Belvedere Palace, built by Prince Eugene of Savoy in the early eighteenth century, consists of two buildings, the Upper and Lower Belvedere, situated at the foot and summit of a gentle hill, with a fine public garden between them. The Lower Belvedere housed the Ambras collection of armour, paintings, jewellery, the Egyptian collection, and portraits of European princes. The Upper Belvedere, referred to here, housed the Imperial Picture Gallery, rich in the Italian and old German masters and ranked second only to Dresden among German art collections. In 1891 the gallery was transferred to the first floor of the Kunsthistorisches Museum.

Grand Terrace: the terrace in front of the Upper Belvedere, 'command[ing] one of the most pleasing views of Vienna' (Murray's *Handbook*).

dogs: andirons, or supports for a fire grate.

20 *an old story*: the legend of Faust, famously retold by Goethe in his verse drama *Faustus* (1808–32).

21 *patent tram-road*: although the first British freight tramway was licensed in 1801, and a horse-drawn passenger tramway of sorts was in operation

in Liverpool in 1858, passenger 'street railways' were not in common use in Britain (unlike France and America) until the end of the century. The first serious experiment came at the start of 1860 when the American entrepreneur George F. Train opened a horse-drawn tramway line in Birkenhead. That same year he petitioned the Board of Trade for permission to open lines in London. By August 1861 he had three lines operating in the city. Though popular with the public, the trams met with fierce opposition from the London General Omnibus Co., and Train was forced to close all his lines by June the following year (Peter Collins, *The Tram Book*, 1995).

21 *thorny wilderness*: the wilderness of the Old Testament, particularly the desert of Arabia where the Israelites spent forty years after the exodus from slavery in Egypt.

double consciousness: a semi-technical term in this period. Physiologists of mind, including Sir Henry Holland (1788–1873), who was to become Eliot and Lewes's friend and occasional consultant physician, hypothesized that the hemispheric structure of the brain had observable consequences for perception. Health of mind depended upon the 'proper correspondence, or unity of action' of the two halves of the brain and nervous system. Injury to, or disease of, the brain could result in a morbid disordering of the thought processes. Sufferers from mental derangement and, in some cases, hysteria were particularly likely to experience 'a sort of double-dealing' of the mind with itself: 'there appear, as it were, two minds; one tending to correct by more just perceptions, feelings, and volitions, the aberrations of the other; and the relative power of these influences varying at different times.' These states, 'where the mind passes by alternation from one state to another, each having the perception of external impressions and appropriate trains of thought, but not linked together by the ordinary gradations, or by mutual memory' were called 'double consciousness' (*Chapters on Mental Physiology*, 1852, 185–7); for discussion see Jane Wood, 'Scientific Rationality and Fanciful Fiction: Gendered Discourse in *The Lifted Veil*', *Women's Writing*, 3/2 (1996), 161–76. Other mid-century writers, including John Addington Symonds, interpreted double consciousness as an associative disorder rather than looking to the structure of the brain for an explanation. See the extract from his *Sleep and Dreams*, and introductory discussion, in Jenny Taylor and Sally Shuttleworth, *Embodied Selves* (1998), sect. 3.

The term also had a specific application within mesmerism. William Gregory used it in *Letters to a Candid Inquirer on Animal Magnetism* (1851) to describe a state in which the mesmeric subject remained in possession of his or her normal waking consciousness while also experiencing the altered consciousness produced by the magnetic state (see Bull, 'Mastery and Slavery in *The Lifted Veil*', p. 250).

Eliot used the term 'double consciousness' of herself on at least two occasions. In her journal account of her visit to Italy in 1860 she wrote that 'One great deduction to me from the delight of seeing world-famous objects is the frequent double consciousness which tells me that I am not enjoying the actual vision enough, and that when higher enjoyment comes with the reproduction of the scene in my imagination I shall have lost some of the details, which impress me too feebly in the present because the faculties are not wrought up into energetic action' (*J* 336). Herbert Spencer noted that she once told him she was 'troubled by double-consciousness—a current of self-criticism being an habitual accompaniment of anything she was saying or doing; and this naturally tended towards self-depreciation and self-distrust' (Spencer, *Autobiography*; quoted in Ashton, *George Eliot*, 220).

22 *which hindered our . . . day*: the *Blackwood's* text reads: 'which hemmed in our generosity, our awe, our human piety, and hindered them from submerging our hard indifference to the sensations and emotions of our fellow. Our tenderness and self-renunciation seem strong when our egoism has had its day—'

the Jews' quarter . . . the old synagogue: the Judenstadt, or Josephstadt, in the old town. Described in Murray's *Handbook* as 'A labyrinth of narrow dirty streets and low houses, swarming with population like an anthill, and estimated to contain about 8000 Jewish inhabitants.' Eliot recorded her own visit to the old synagogue and the Jewish burial ground in very similar terms to Latimer's in her journal (*J* 324).

cicerone: guide.

26 *Tasso*: Torquato Tasso (1544–95), author of the epic poem, *Gerusalemme Liberata*, was declared insane and imprisoned by Alphonso d'Este II from 1579 to 1586. Goethe, Byron, and Shelley all contributed to a Romantic cult of Tasso. Eliot read Goethe's verse play *Torquato Tasso* (1790) in Berlin in 1854 (*J* 38–9), but Latimer would no doubt be more drawn to Byron's 'The Lament of Tasso', which focuses more sharply on the legendary tale that the poet's love for Leonora d'Este led to his imprisonment by the duke.

29 *adytum*: the most sacred part of the temple; the shrine or chancel.

hashish: infusion of Indian hemp, used as a narcotic.

33 *incubus*: an evil demon or fairy. Often used of the oppressiveness of nightmare.

38 *peritonitis*: inflammation of the peritoneum or membrane lining the cavity of the abdomen. In this period the term covered a range of ailments of the stomach and bowel. In terminal cases the sufferer experienced acute pain, and death occurred within a few days.

40 *peignoir*: a loose dressing gown.

42 *Great God! Is this what it is to live again*: 'Good God! This is what it is to live again' in the *Blackwood's* text. See Introduction, p. xxvi.

BROTHER JACOB

46 *Epigraph*: 'Deceivers all I write for you, | Measure for measure waits you too' (Robert Thomson (trans.), *La Fontaine's Fables* (Paris, 1806), i. 30). A more literal translation would be, 'Deceivers, I write for you: | Await the same fate'. This moral concludes La Fontaine's fable of 'The Fox and the Stork' in which the fox invites the stork to dine and tricks her out of her meal by serving broth on a plate from which, with her long beak, she cannot sup. She retaliates by inviting him to dinner and serving meat in a vase with a narrow mouth. The surname of Eliot's antihero, Faux, echoes 'fox' (as Eliot points out at the end of the story) and means 'false'.

49 *yeoman*: historically, a freeholder below the rank of gentleman. More broadly, a commoner or countryman of respectable standing.

macaroons . . . marengs . . . twelfth-cake: macaroons are small sweet cakes made chiefly from almonds, egg whites, and sugar. Mareng is a variant spelling of meringue. A twelfth-cake is a rich cake or bun originally baked for Twelfth Night. Usually frosted and containing a 'bean' or coin, the finder of which becomes the king or queen of the feast.

doctrine of the Inconceivable: a reference to the debate about inconceivability which occupied several leading British philosophers during the 1850s, among them William Whewell, John Stuart Mill, Herbert Spencer, Sir William Hamilton, and his disciple Henry Longueville Mansel. The debate concerned a problem in associationist psychology regarding whether or not there are 'necessary truths' uncompromised by our perception of them. In his *A System of Logic* (1843), Mill—the great leader of the 'empirical' as opposed to what he called the 'intuitional school' of philosophers—had taken issue with Whewell's claim that 'Necessary truths are those in which . . . the negation of the truth is not only false, but impossible; in which we cannot, even by an effort of imagination, or in a supposition, conceive the reverse of that which is asserted' (*Philosophy of the Inductive Sciences*, 1840, i. 54.). Mill responded: 'I cannot but wonder that so much stress should be laid on the circumstance of inconceivableness, when there is ample experience to show that our capacity or incapacity of conceiving a thing has very little to do with the possibility of the thing in itself' (p. 313). He adduced the gradual acceptance, throughout the history of science, of ideas which previous generations found 'inconceivable'. Spencer disagreed, arguing in an essay in the *Westminster Review* (Oct. 1853; rpt. as ch. 1 of *Principles of Psychology*, 1855) that such cases were really ones of error, in which experience had not yet warranted belief in the concepts proposed. The article prompted a rebuttal from Mill in the next edition of *Logic*, and an ongoing argument which led to a friendship.

The other major figure in the debate is the Scottish philosopher Sir William Hamilton, with whom Spencer had also taken issue. Hamilton, in the 'Supplementary Dissertations' appended to his 1852 edition of Thomas Reid's *Works*, had rejected inconceivability. He offered the example of our inability to conceive of space and time either as ultimately bounded or as without limit, arguing that one of these two propositions must be true but that the inconceivability test could result only in 'contradictory inconceivables'—that is, in the absurd statement that space both has and has not a limit. Spencer retorted, 'How do we *know* that it is impossible for the same thing to be and not to be?' Hamilton expanded on his views in *Lectures on Metaphysics and Logic*, 4 vols. (1859–60) where he set out his doctrine of the phenomenal and relative status of all knowledge, urging that we cannot have access to ultimate reality because knowledge is always coloured by the mind. If we attempt to do so we are left with contradictory inconceivables—the Absolute (that is, limited) and the Infinite—one of which must be true. We therefore accept the alternative justified by our 'moral and religious feelings'. Hamilton had modified Kant's account of pure reason in a way which safeguarded his own religious faith, though some of his opponents, Spencer among them, would go on to argue that the logical outcome of this philosophical standpoint was agnosticism. The inconceivability test is summarized in Spencer's 'Universal Postulate': *'a belief which is proved by the inconceivableness of its negation to invariably exist, is true.'* We have, he concluded, 'no other guarantee for the reality of consciousness, of sensations, of personal existence'.

Eliot read Spencer's chapter on 'The Universal Postulate' when it was first published in article form in the *Westminster Review* (Oct. 1856) and suggested a revision which she gratefully adopted for the book (see George Eliot, *The George Eliot Letters*, ed. Gordon S. Haight, 9 vols. (New Haven, 1954–78), hereafter cited as *L*, ii. 145). She had made a gift of Mill's *System of Logic* to him in 1852, so that he credited her with having introduced him to Mill's writing on the Universal Postulate. Her knowledge of Hamilton is recorded in a letter she wrote to Sara Hennell in July 1861, recalling her admiration for 'an article on Sir William Hamilton's doctrine of contradictory inconceivables' which had appeared in the *Saturday Review* in 1859 (13 August, 196–8) (see *L* iii. 438).

The specific phrasing, *'doctrine* of the Inconceivable', may indicate an additional side-swipe at the doctrine of the Immaculate Conception of the Blessed Virgin Mary, announced by Pope Pius IX on 8 December 1854 and published in a Papal Bull 'Ineffabilis Deus'. The pronouncement (requiring all Catholics to accept that the Blessed Virgin Mary, 'by the singular privilege and grace of the omnipotent God', was 'preserved immaculate from all stain of original sin') was fiercely debated in Britain, as across Europe. The leading opponent of the doctrine from within the Catholic Church, the French Abbé Laborde, published his objections to the Vatican's procedures, and was consequently placed on the 'Index' of blacklisted books at Rome. See *Quarterly Review*, 97 (1855), 143–83.

Brigford: Eliot may have known of the old village of East Brigford in Nottingham but it is more likely that this place name, like the majority in 'Brother Jacob', was intended to be fictional.

50 *Mechanics' Institute*: the first of these societies to promote popular education through the provision of classes and lectures was established by
George Birkbeck in Glasgow in 1823. London followed in 1824, and over
the next two decades Institutes were formed in most major British towns
and cities. Their principal, though not exclusive, focus was on the
sciences.

'Inkle and Yarico': in the *Spectator*, Tuesday 13 March 1711, Richard
Steele told the story of a beautiful native American Indian woman,
Yarico, who saved the life of a young London merchant, Thomas Inkle,
only to be taken by him to Barbados and sold into slavery. When she
pleaded with him that she was carrying his child he used the information to drive up her sale price. Steele was embroidering a story from
Richard Ligon's *A True and Exact History of the Island of Barbados*
(London, 1657). The name 'Inkle' was his invention. There were
numerous eighteenth-century adaptations of the story, among them
George Colman Jr's musical play *Inkle and Yarico* (1787) which was
performed very successfully at Covent Garden and at the Haymarket.
Beryl Gray suggests that, if Eliot did not know the Colman version
through G. H. Lewes, a keen theatre-goer, reviewer, and actor, she may
have come across it in volume 16 of *Cumberland's British Theatre*, by
John Cumberland (1829).

51 *beans*: from the French *biens*, goods.

52 *Chubb's patent*: the first Chubb lock was patented by Charles Chubb
(1773–1845) in 1818, with improved designs registered in 1824, 1828, and
1833. His son, John Chubb (1816–72) was awarded the silver Telford
medal of the Institution of Civil Engineers in 1851 for his work tracing all
British patents relating to locks and keys.

third Sunday in Lent: depending on the year, either early March or the very
end of February.

53 *mens nil conscia sibi*: literally, 'a mind not conscious of itself'; more loosely,
'a mind without guilty conscience' or 'a mind without self-knowledge'.
Possibly a misquotation of Virgil, *Aeneid*, i. 604: 'mens sibi conscia recti',
'a mind conscious of rectitude' (the 'learned friend' whose name must
be suppressed being clearly less learned than he pretends). The phrase
comes from Aeneas' first address to Dido, Queen of Carthage: 'if any
divine powers have regard for good, if justice has any weight anywhere,
may the gods and the consciousness of right, bring thee worthy rewards.'
Alternatively, Eliot may have intended an allusion to Horace's urging of
the advantages of a clear conscience in his *Epistolae* I. i. 60: 'Hic murus
aeneos esto | Nil conscire sibi, nulla pallescere culpa', 'Let this be as a
brazen wall of defence, to be conscious of no guilt, to turn pale at no
accusations.'

Louis Napoleon: (1808–73). Nephew of Napoleon Bonaparte and, as
Napoleon III, Emperor of France, 1852–70. Britain's alliance with Louis
Napoleon had been tested by his prosecution of an Italian war, in support

of the nationalist movement, in the late 1850s. A free-trade agreement was signed by the two countries in 1860, despite the opposition of the French bourgeoisie.

Caliban . . . Trinculo's wine: Shakespeare, *The Tempest*, II. ii.

54 *Sally Lunn*: a sweet, light tea-cake, usually served hot. Named after the woman who supposedly first sold them in Bath. Put to comic use in Robert Barnabas Brough's historical drama *King Alfred and the Cakes* (1852) where Alfred is made to intone: 'Behold this Sally Lunn!' Also the subject of a comic song a few years after 'Brother Jacob' in W. S. Gilbert's *The Merry Zingara, or the Tipsy Gipsy and the Popsy Wopsy* (1868): 'Toast now the tea-cake peerlessly! Sally Lunn, the Sally, Sally Lunn, Sally Lunn!'

not having studied the psychology of idiots: a reference to the growing literature on idiocy at mid-century, notably Saul Gridley Howe's report on idiocy in Massachusetts (*On the Causes of Idiocy*, 1848), discussed by Harriet Martineau in an article for *Household Words* in 1854 ('Idiots Again', *HW* 9, 15 April 1854, 197–200). The piece was in part a follow-up to one by Dickens and W. H. Wills in June 1853 describing Dr Guggenbühl's mountain clinic in Switzerland, where a combination of moral management and education had produced remarkable advances in the capabilities of idiot children. The most notable figure on the British scene at this time was Dr John Langdon Down, whose Idiot Asylum at Earlswood, Surrey, was established on similar principles to Guggenbühl's in 1853, though Down's major published contributions to the field would not start appearing until the mid-1860s. See Introduction, pp. xxxii–xxxiii.

56 *astute heroes of M. de Balzac*: the french novelist Honoré de Balzac, regularly attacked by Victorian reviewers as a corrupter of morals and a poor stylist. The *Westminster Review*, under Eliot's editorship, had defended him and she herself described him in an essay on Goethe's *Wilhelm Meister* as 'perhaps the most wonderful writer of fiction the world has ever seen' (George Eliot, *Essays of George Eliot*, ed. Thomas Pinney (New York, 1963), 146, hereafter cited as *Essays*). However, when she read *Le Père Goriot* in October 1855 she thought it 'a hateful book' (*J* 81). Of the heroes in works she is known to have read— *Eugénie Grandet* (1833), *Goriot* (1835), *Illusions perdues* (1837–9), *César Birotteau* (1838), and *Mémoires de deux jeunes mariées* (1841)—the description seems best suited to Eugène in *Goriot* and Vautrin in *Illusions perdues*.

57 *cats*: almost certainly a reference to the demand for cats in order to keep down rodent infestations in various colonies. On 19 May 1851 *The Times* reported that 100 cats had also been imported into San Francisco for that purpose. The West Indies had long suffered from the depredations of rodents. On 11 November 1808 *The Times* reported that 50,000 rats were being destroyed annually on some Jamaican plantations without 'any sensible diminution of their numbers' and at an estimated cost of 8–10 out of every 100 hogsheads of sugar.

57 *horse-block*: small platform, usually of stone and with two or more steps, from which one mounted a horse.

60 *The ways of thieving were not ways of pleasantness*: an ironic allusion to the praise of wisdom in Proverbs 3: 17: 'Her ways are ways of pleasantness, and all her paths are peace.'

Gorgon or Demogorgon: the gorgons were the three mythical females with snakes for hair, whose glance turned the viewer to stone. The most famous is Medusa, who was slain by Perseus and her head affixed to Athene's shield. The mysterious and infernal female deity the demogorgon can be found in, amongst others, Spenser's *Faerie Queene*, IV. ii, Milton's *Paradise Lost*, ii. 962, and Shelley's *Prometheus Unbound*, Act II.

61 *Church-people ... Dissenters*: 'Dissenters' is an umbrella term, including the Quakers, Independents (or Congregationalists), Baptists, Presbyterians and Unitarians, the many varieties of Methodism—most notably Primitive Methodism—and numerous smaller groupings outside the established Church of England. It should not be taken to embrace Evangelical Anglicanism. In general, Dissent was associated with low social standing in Victorian England, and the Anglican establishment remained largely unmoved by the legal penalties of Nonconformity (though the law was changed in 1837 to permit marriages to take place in dissenting chapels, the burial laws were not amended until 1880; Oxford and Cambridge did not fully open their doors to Dissenters until well into the twentieth century). Many Victorian novels represent accurately enough the social and cultural divide between Anglicanism and Dissent, but Eliot's are unusual for their sympathetic and informed portrayal of Nonconformity—so much so that she felt the need to protect herself from the charge of hostility to Anglicanism, for all her break with organized Christianity. She wrote to Gertrude Lewes in 1865: 'I was brought up in the Church of England, and never belonged to any other religious body. I care that this should be known ... as I have been, and perhaps shall be, depicting dissenters with much sympathy' (*L* iv. 213). In fact the parodic Dissenters' names (Mr Rodd, the Baptist minister; Zephania Crypt, the defunct charity school benefactor) make 'Brother Jacob' an uncharacteristically satirical presentation of Nonconformity.

a late visitation by commissioners: the first half of the nineteenth century saw several commissions of inquiry into education, including the 1834 Commission on the State of Education of the People.

Yellow Coat School: a joking reference to the Blue Coat, Green Coat, and Black Coat Charity schools, so named because of the regulation robes worn by the pupils. The most famous was Christ's Hospital in London, where the boys wore a long dark-blue gown fastened at the waist with a belt, and bright yellow stockings. On Easter Monday of every year they processed to the Mansion House where each boy received a glass of wine, a bun, and a shilling from the Lord Mayor.

China-asters: flowers (*Callistephus chinensis*) with large radiated daisy blooms. Related to the Michaelmas Daisy. The reference is to the new fashion for elaborate window-dressing.

62 *jobbed linen*: bought on the cheap from a bulk-dealer (i.e. a job lot).

the shutters were taken down: shop fronts were covered at night by tall wooden shutters, slotted into a groove under the architrave and, usually, carried in and out by the apprentices at the beginning and end of each day. Roller shutters, made of iron ribs, were first introduced in the late 1830s and rapidly gained in popularity. The wooden shutters on Edward Freely's fashionable new shop, together with the reference to Mechanics' Institutes, places his story some time before the 1830s.

collared and marbled meats: collared meats are cuts from which the bones have been removed and which are then rolled and tied with string. Collared pork, recommended by Mrs Beeton as a breakfast dish, was composed of cuts from the face, head, ears, and feet of the pig, boiled then cut into small pieces and pressed into the shape of a roll, with the skin laid round. Collared meats might also be pickled. Marbled meats are lean cuts veined with thin layers of fat (a sign of the best quality).

Dutch painter: a reference to the Dutch tradition of intensely observed realism, more than once invoked in Eliot's essays and reviews as a model for fiction writing.

63 *Turner's latest style*: the reference could be either to the landscapes of the late 1820s and early 1830s which Ruskin had defended in the first volume of *Modern Painters* (1843), or to the almost abstract evocations of light and colour from the later 1830s and 1840s for which J. M. W. Turner (1775–1851) is now most famous.

Punch . . . market-place: the Punch and Judy man setting up his puppet-booth.

mazarine: deep rich blue.

manna-gift: food miraculously supplied to the children of Israel during their journey through the wilderness; Exodus 16: 14–15.

hidden law of sequence: a reference to the causal laws of thought as expounded by philosophers, e.g. Herbert Spencer, *First Principles* (1862), ii, ch. 3, § 47: 'Relations of which the terms are not reversible become recognized as sequences proper; while relations of which the terms occur indifferently in both directions, become recognized as co-existences.'

64 *carding mill*: a mill where wool was 'dressed' or prepared for spinning by being combed and teased in carding-machines.

ratafias: biscuits or cakes flavoured with ratafia, a cordial distilled from molasses and flavoured with fruits or their kernels—usually almond, cherry, peach, or apricot kernels.

peripateia: (peripeteia) a sudden change or reversal of fortune. A defining characteristic of tragedy in Aristotle's *Poetics*.

'Lalla Rookh', the 'Corsair', and the 'Siege of Corinth': 'Lalla Rookh' was a

popular oriental ballad by Thomas Moore (1817). 'The Corsair' (1814) and 'The Siege of Corinth' (1816), both by Byron, were largely responsible for fashioning the Regency taste for oriental verse tales.

64 *'bulbul'*: the Persian nightingale of romances.

spavin: a swelling or hard lump growing on the inside of a horse's hind leg, near the joint, causing lameness. Usually produced by inflammation of the cartilage.

renegade: a Christian who becomes a Muslim or, more broadly, a deserter from one cause or principle in favour of another—as in Moore's *Lalla Rookh*: 'Must he . . . be driven | A renegade like me from Love and Heaven' ('Veiled Prophet', 690).

66 *division of labour*: the term put into general currency by Adam Smith's *An Enquiry into the Nature and Causes of the Wealth of Nations* (1776), indicating specialization of work.

calcareous: containing calcium carbonate (lime). See Introduction, p. xxxiv.

that young lady of the 'Spectator's' acquaintance: 'Sabine Rentfree' in Richard Steele's *Spectator*, 15 July 1712, describes how 'one Day playing with a Tobacco-pipe between my Teeth, it happened to break in my Mouth, and spitting out the Pieces left such a delicious Roughness on my Tongue, that I could not be satisfied till I had champ'd up the remaining Part of the Pipe. I . . . stuck to the Pipes three Months, in which Time I had dispenc'd with 37 foul Piles, all to the Boles.' She then progresses to chalk, stones, half a foot of garden wall, and coal, until cured by marriage of what she describes as a clear case of the 'Green-sickness'.

67 *the Palfreys*: a palfrey is a small horse suitable for ladies.

charm the ears of Grimworth Desdemonas: as Othello charmed Desdemona with stories of his adventures, *Othello*, I. iii. 128–68.

mercer: dealer in textile fabrics and fine cloths.

68 *an overseer of the poor*: under the old Poor Law—that is, before 1834—overseers were responsible for the poor law accounts, and had the principal say in how much relief was offered to a pauper. The diarist Thomas Turner described his duties as an overseer in East Hoathly, Sussex, in the 1750s and 1760s. They included paying out doles, dealing with vagrants and settlement cases, keeping bills and vouchers, getting his accounts approved by the justices and his pensions by the vestry. An overseer might have to appear before a justice to show why he had refused a person relief, and to defend the parish against charges of being 'hard to our poor'. The more common charges, however, related to their overspending the parish budget. Overseers were widely distrusted, and complaints about their partiality, misconduct, and laxity mounted from the 1660s until the Poor Law Amendment Act of 1834. (*The Diary of Thomas Turner 1754–1765*, 1984, Paul Slack, *The English Poor Law, 1531–1782*, 1990.)

a world which has long been flat and stale to them: an allusion to *Hamlet's* first soliloquy, I. ii. 133–4:

> How weary, stale, flat, and unprofitable
> Seem to me all the uses of this world!

69 *the Ideal . . . the Real*: Eliot perhaps had half an eye on Herbert Spencer's concept of ideal beauty. In an article entitled 'Personal Beauty', published in the *Leader* (15 April and 13 May 1854), he endorsed the classical Greek head of harmonious proportions and condemned prominent or fleshy noses, jaws, mouths, and upper lips. His views were acutely wounding to Eliot, who was painfully conscious of her own want of beauty.

crop: the fashion for young girls wearing their hair in short (around shoulder-length) curls gradually went out during the 1840s and 1850s. In Dickens's *Martin Chuzzlewit* (1843–4), Cherry Pecksniff wears her hair in a 'loosely flowing crop'.

murrain: a plague-like disease of cattle. There were repeated bad outbreaks in the first half of the nineteenth century, notably in Scotland in the winter of 1840–1, and across the Continent and in Britain in January 1845. Reports of an outbreak in Holstein in early 1857 prompted emergency measures to restrict the importation of cattle. See *The Times*, 13 April 1857, p. 9 a, and 25 April 1857, p. 9 f.

70 *Captain Cook*: James Cook (1728–79), circumnavigator and explorer. On a voyage to Tahiti in 1769 he observed the Transit of Venus and charted New Zealand, the east coast of Australia, and parts of New Guinea. On later voyages he passed across the highest southern ice-floes of the Antarctic, and charted many of the Pacific islands.

Mangnall's Questions: *Historical and Miscellaneous Questions for the Use of Young People*, by the Yorkshire schoolmistress Richmal Mangnall (1769–1820), was first published anonymously in 1800. She sold the copyright to Longman and by 1818 the book had been through fourteen editions and numerous reprintings.

'Without thee, it is pain to live, | *But with thee, it were sweet to die'*: unidentified. (Mudford suggests an allusion to Keble's hymn 'Sun of My Soul, Thou Saviour Dear' (1827), but the likeness is too remote.)

72 *K.C.B.*: Knight Commander of the Bath. The Order of the Bath was enlarged in 1815 and further extended in 1847 with the addition of the Civil Branch (i.e. the KCB Civil was added to the existing KCB Military).

Nelson: Horatio, Viscount Nelson (1758–1805), commemorated by Nelson's Column, Trafalgar Square. Celebrated British admiral, victorious over the French fleet in the Battle of the Nile (1798) and over the Danish navy at Copenhagen (1801), but best known for his victory over the French in the battle of Trafalgar Bay (1805). He died at Trafalgar.

72 *Titian*: Titiano Vecellio. Famous Italian painter (*c.*1490–1576).

74 *the great Leviathan*: the biblical monster of the deep. The reference is to Job 41: 1: 'Cans't thou draw out leviathan with an hook?' Eliot is drawing on the word's Hobbesian application to the state or the *res publica*.

80 *to make a slip . . . lip*: playing on the English proverb 'There's many a slip 'twixt cup and lip'.

87 *peculium*: under Roman Law, the property which a father allowed his child, or a master his slave, to hold as his own; hence, private, or exclusive, property.

JANE AUSTEN	Emma
	Persuasion
	Pride and Prejudice
	Sense and Sensibility
MRS BEETON	Book of Household Management
ANNE BRONTË	The Tenant of Wildfell Hall
CHARLOTTE BRONTË	Jane Eyre
EMILY BRONTË	Wuthering Heights
WILKIE COLLINS	The Moonstone
	The Woman in White
JOSEPH CONRAD	Heart of Darkness and Other Tales
	Nostromo
CHARLES DARWIN	The Origin of Species
CHARLES DICKENS	Bleak House
	David Copperfield
	Great Expectations
	Hard Times
GEORGE ELIOT	Middlemarch
	The Mill on the Floss
ELIZABETH GASKELL	Cranford
THOMAS HARDY	Jude the Obscure
	Tess of the d'Urbervilles
WALTER SCOTT	Ivanhoe
MARY SHELLEY	Frankenstein
ROBERT LOUIS STEVENSON	Treasure Island
BRAM STOKER	Dracula
WILLIAM MAKEPEACE THACKERAY	Vanity Fair
OSCAR WILDE	The Picture of Dorian Gray

TROLLOPE IN OXFORD WORLD'S CLASSICS

ANTHONY TROLLOPE

An Autobiography

The American Senator

Barchester Towers

Can You Forgive Her?

The Claverings

Cousin Henry

Doctor Thorne

The Duke's Children

The Eustace Diamonds

Framley Parsonage

He Knew He Was Right

Lady Anna

The Last Chronicle of Barset

Orley Farm

Phineas Finn

Phineas Redux

The Prime Minister

Rachel Ray

The Small House at Allington

The Warden

The Way We Live Now

The Oxford World's Classics Website

www.worldsclassics.co.uk

- Information about new titles
- Explore the full range of Oxford World's Classics
- Links to other literary sites and the main OUP webpage
- Imaginative competitions, with bookish prizes
- Peruse the Oxford World's Classics Magazine
- Articles by editors
- Extracts from Introductions
- A forum for discussion and feedback on the series
- Special information for teachers and lecturers

www.worldsclassics.co.uk

American Literature

British and Irish Literature

Children's Literature

Classics and Ancient Literature

Colonial Literature

Eastern Literature

European Literature

History

Medieval Literature

Oxford English Drama

Poetry

Philosophy

Politics

Religion

The Oxford Shakespeare

A complete list of Oxford Paperbacks, including Oxford World's Classics, Oxford Shakespeare, Oxford Drama, and Oxford Paperback Reference, is available in the UK from the Academic Division Publicity Department, Oxford University Press, Great Clarendon Street, Oxford OX2 6DP.

In the USA, complete lists are available from the Paperbacks Marketing Manager, Oxford University Press, 198 Madison Avenue, New York, NY 10016.

Oxford Paperbacks are available from all good bookshops. In case of difficulty, customers in the UK can order direct from Oxford University Press Bookshop, Freepost, 116 High Street, Oxford OX1 4BR, enclosing full payment. Please add 10 per cent of published price for postage and packing.